MORRISTON 1885.

I enjoyed working in my shop, meeting new customers and chatting with my regular ones. On busy days the time passed quickly and it seemed that I was shutting up shop only shortly after opening it! Those days were the better days, the quieter ones were not so good. Time tended to hang heavy on my shoulders when custom was scarce. There are only so many times you can re-arrange the goods display, clean the counter tops and sweep the floor. I just wish the shop was in another part of the country. Where the air is cleaner and the views much better.

My grandfather started the business years ago and when he died it should have gone to my father. Grandfather told me that my dad never took any interest in the shop and that as soon as he was old enough he went to work in the copper factory. Sadly, my father was killed in an industrial accident when I was a small boy.

The shop is situated on Clase Road in the industrial town of Morriston, a town built to the east of Swansea which is a very busy coastal town in South West Wales. Swansea was built on trade via its large dock complex, ships laden with goods constantly entering and leaving. Swansea's main export is high grade copper much treasured throughout the world for its quality. The copper is manufactured on a huge industrial scale in factories that run along the banks of the river Tawe, from St Thomas, eastwards, as far as Morriston.

The vast industrial sprawl is known as Copperopolis. A dark and dirty place that employs many of the men of the area and has also killed many men. Coal mines are numerous and employ those men that the copper works cannot. Copperopolis is a coal eating monster, always hungry and always being fed, ton after ton of coal thrown into its hungry jaws.

I sometimes stood outside the shop and looked at the forests of tall factory chimneys belching out black and noxious smoke that discolours all that it touches and poisons the land and the water. Very little grew as the soil was too heavily polluted with whatever substances were spewed out by the chimneys and fell to the ground. It was only on the higher ground away from the smoke that the dead land turned green again.

In summer time, on the rare occasion that the sun shone in a sky of blue, it was obscured by the grey haze that permanently covered the area like a misty blanket. I didn't like it here anymore. I was beginning to hate it. I was constantly reminded of the fact that copperopolis killed my father.

One morning I decided that now was time to sell up and move on. I was not married and had no children. I had no brothers or sisters and no family ties to keep me here. My mother had left my dad and I many years ago when I was just a toddler. To his dying day my dad had no idea why she left or where she had gone....she simply vanished!

I asked my grandfather many times about my mother. His reply was always the same. "She left, that's all you need to know, Rees bach, upped sticks and disappeared. Broke your dad's heart she did. Now, don't ask me any more questions about it, you understand?"

Of course, I did ask, again and again and again. Until my grandfather made it very clear that I mustn't ask again.

"Rees! For the love of, no more questions about your mother. There were rumours of something bad going on. After she disappeared the gossips got to making up tales, as they do. Nasty tales at that, tales that you don't want to hear. It was along time ago now, Bach. Let sleeping dogs lie."

I never asked him again. It was very hard for me but sometimes the past is best left in the past.

On the morning of my decision to leave I was talking to one of my long standing customers, John Kelly. He came into the shop every couple of days or so for his pipe tobacco. I stocked his favourite, Cherry flavour. John said he was a manager at the Dyffryn metal works, a nice man who never said a bad word about anyone. About fifty five years old, with grey hair which was beginning to recede. Steel grey eyes which peered out of a plump face that always appeared to be smiling. He always wore a bright paisley three piece suit. A gold watch chain visible on his waist coat. A pair of brightly polished shoes showed below the hem line of his trousers. He never wore a hat, which I thought strange as most men in his position did.

"London, Rees, that's the place to be. The largest commercial city in the world. Open a shop there and you'll make a fortune. I know you don't do so bad here but London is the place. More classier clientele see."

"Not sure about that John. London is a long way away. Not sure I want to go that far. I was thinking more like Cardiff."

"Why would you want to go to Cardiff? May as-well stay here as go to bloody Cardiff, Rees. I have a cousin up in London, he knows a lot of people who know people, if you see what I mean. I'll have a word with him. Can't do any harm, Rees. Hold on a little while longer until I get word from him. If you're in a hurry then you'd best get on with it but I know my cousin can help."

"I'm not in a desperate hurry, John, I just need a change, to get away from this dirty little town and away from the memories it holds."

"Right you are then, I'll write immediately. It will take a week or two to get a reply. Bye for now, Rees."

John was right. Cardiff wasn't an option, it would be much the same as Morriston. I needed a new start and London could be it.

John didn't come into the shop for nearly a fortnight, which was very unusual. I was starting to wonder if he had forgotten our conversation when I heard the shop door open and in he came. Talk of the devil, or should that be think of the devil? He seemed rather flustered or over excited. I couldn't decide which.

"Hello, Rees, how are you?" He reached over the counter to shake my hand. Strange I thought, he's never done that before.

"I've got some good news for you. My cousin has pulled a few strings with some of the people he knows. There is an empty shop in Spitalfields, very posh area of London that is, Rees. He has even sorted the legal side out for you. The contract is ready, all you have to do is sign it."

"Bloody hell, John, that was quick. I thought it would take weeks, all that legal stuff usually does."

"Depends on who you know, doesn't it. My cousin, Jack McCarthy, will be sending me all the details including the contract. There will be a fee involved but that's a small price to pay when all the work is done for you."

"I'll need to get the contract looked at by my solicitor, John, just to make sure all is above board."

John Kelly looked at me as if I had punched him!

"I'm hurt by that, Rees. How long have you known me? I can vouch for my cousin, he is a good man. He has a business himself. Why spend more money when you don't have to? I can assure you that it will be all above board but if that's what you want to do it's fine by me."

John was right, I'd never known him speak ill of anyone. He was friendly to all that he met. I'd never heard an ill word spoken against him either.

"Alright, John. Forgive me, years of business dealings you know. Drop the contract in when you get it."

"Thank You, Rees. I should get the information and the contract within a fortnight or so. I'll be seeing you."

He left the shop rather briskly and I couldn't help but feel a pang of guilt for hurting his feelings.

I went about my day to day activities associated with the life of a shop keeper. Greeting my customers, a little banter with some, more of a conversation with others. Bad news greeted me one day, Jones The Fish, he owned a fishmongers in Woodfield Street, came rushing into the shop.

"Have you heard the news, Rees? Terrible it is, there's been an explosion in one of the furnaces in White Rock. Many men killed, they don't know exactly how many yet."

"No, that's awful, Mr Jones. When did this happen?"

"Just now, Rees, come have a look out here, you can see the smoke."

Over in the distance, I could see a massive column of thick red/black smoke rising into the air, like the foetid breath of a fearsome dragon. Copperopolis claims the lives of more of its inhabitants. Any nagging doubts I had about leaving left me that day.

"Let me know how I can help, Mr Jones."

"I will lad, most likely start a disaster fund, food and the like. You can help out there, Rees." And he trotted off up Woodfield Street and back to his fish shop.

The conversation over the next few days was all about the disaster. Poor Mrs so and so now a widow. Mrs so and so lost her son etc. All very depressing. Those of us that could helped those affected by the disaster and there were many.

Copperopolis kept going, the damaged furnace was closed down but the remainder were working at full blast. Night and day they operated trying to make up for the loss of their fallen brother. The wealthy owners sitting safely at home in their plush houses in the more affluent areas to the west of Swansea. Areas where the smoke doesn't reach and the grass is green.

On a very wet and windy morning in early March, John Kelly blustered into my shop, cursing the weather, looking around as he did so. I presumed that he didn't want to offend any customers that may have been waiting to be served. Luckily, he was the only one in the shop at the time.

"This bloody weather will be the death of me! March, my arse, more like November!"

He removed his sodden overcoat and shook it out. Water droplets sprayed everywhere. He fished frantically in one of its pockets, cursing as his fingers missed their intended target. Eventually he retrieved a large manilla envelope and placed it on the counter top.

"Here we are, Rees, all the documentation is here. And the contract of course. I'll pop into the cafe over the road for a hot cup of tea while you get stuck into that lot."

He donned his coat and left the shop. I watched as he crossed the road and headed towards the cafe. The wind playing games with his un-buttoned coat, causing it to bellow out behind him like a phantom cape.

I picked up the envelope and took out its contents. Numerous sheets of print lay before me. Details of the premises, terms of use, vacant and ready for new tenant.

All that you would expect to see concerning a property you were to lease. And the contract. I read through the lines of print, all seemed to be in-order, just my signature required. I then noticed the fee, ten pounds! That was a hell of a lot of money.

Some time later, John entered the shop. A lot drier as the rain had stopped but he was just a tad wind blown.

"Have you read through it all? Everything above board and to your liking?"

"Yes, it all looks to be in-order, except for the fee. Ten pounds, John. That is a lot of money."

"Not really, Rees, you have to take into account that certain palms had to be crossed with silver, so to speak, to get it done so quickly. And my cousin has included his fee of course. If you had done it all yourself it would have taken much longer."

He was right, I was just a little shocked to see the figures.

"Ready to sign the contract then? Oh, and I'll need the fee in cash, Rees. I'll pay it into my bank and they can wire my cousins bank in London. Then its all done and dusted." John gave me one of his beaming smiles. I couldn't help but smile back.

I went upstairs to my bedroom where I kept my strong box. Using the key that I kept tied around my neck I attempted to open the box.

It was a stubborn lock, stubborn and lazy, wouldn't turn and didn't want to turn! Eventually, with a loud click, the box opened. I counted out the notes, folded them up and placed them in my pocket.

On returning downstairs and entering the shop area I found John sitting on an upturned packing case, puffing away on his pipe. The tobacco smoke smelled of cherry, very sweet.

"Buying your tobacco elsewhere then, John?" I asked.

"Not by choice, Rees. Been out of town a lot recently, business, you know how it is."

"I was wondering where you'd got to." I replied.

" Let's get the contract signed then and start the wheels in motion." John said enthusiastically.

I signed the contract and handed it and the cash to John. He didn't bother counting it, just placed the folded notes into his coat pocket.

"John, we need two witnesses to sign this as-well."

"Not to worry there, Rees. I'll get a couple of the men from the office to sign. No problem."

" I suppose you want a receipt for the cash." John said. Not a question but a statement. I could have sworn he had a challenging look on his face.

"No, John. I trust you. I would like a copy of the contract though, If you have one that is?"

"Er, no, I don't, Rees. I'll get onto McCarthy, he can send me a copy for you." He flashed me his amiable smile, doffed his imaginary hat and left the shop, battling the wind as he crossed the road and made his way up Woodfield Street.

On the day the for sale sign went up on the shop front I had many sad customers standing at the counter. One was old Nelly Phillips, a widow, her husband a victim of Copperopolis. A grey haired, wrinkly faced, short and stout woman, who walked slowly and with a stoop as if she had the weight of the world on her shoulders. The truth is that she probably felt that she did. She came in every day for her bread, a little butter, bacon, eggs and a few sausages. Never any fish or proper meat, her purse didn't stretch to such extravagances. Very often I would 'forget' to charge for the bread, or I would add an extra sausage or two and the same for the bacon. She knew I did it but always smiled and said I was a kind man with a heart of gold.

Little Timmy Jenkins was another regular, every morning before school, he was one of the few that went to school, he would call in for his halfpenny of boiled sweets. There were the odd days when he would stand outside the shop and look through the window. I knew then that he didn't have the halfpenny. I would weigh out the sweets, place them in a paper bag and give it to him. My reward was the huge smile that lit up his face and to be told that I was a 'goodun' "You're a goodun Mr Llewellyn" he would shout as he ran off to school.

Dai the coal merchant or 'Dai The Coal' as he was known came every morning for a packet of Woodbine cigarettes. I wondered how he managed to smoke them as he constantly coughed. A victim to the dust of his trade. Despite his appearance, Dai was a relatively wealthy man and didn't need any assistance from me.

I had many customers, too numerous to mention, that I helped out by forgetting to charge for this and adding a little extra of that. My more affluent customers financed that little arrangement; they always paid full price and received no extras.

The for sale sign had been up for a week or so when a man came into the shop who I didn't recognise, new to town I thought. He was having a good look around.

The Davies sisters came in just after him. Two of the dearest people I have ever met. Neither of them had married and they were inseparable. They went every where together.

"Morning, Rees, bach" said Evelyn, the elder sister. "How are you this fine morning? Keeping well I hope."

"Good morning, Evelyn. Good morning Agnes. How may I help you?

Evelyn was trying to read from what looked like her shopping list. Moving the piece of paper closer and then further away from her eyes, trying to focus the words written on it. "Give to me!" Agnes, the younger sister exclaimed. "Blind as a bat you are girl. You wouldn't see a tree until you walked into it!"

"I am not blind! My eyes are watering from the cold, that's all." Evelyn said, rather indignantly.

Agnes duly called out the items written on the list and I retrieved them and placed them in the basket which Evelyn had placed on the counter. All the time the man was inspecting the shop, looking at this and peering into that. I had one eye on the job and the other eye on this strange, nosey man.

"There we are, Rees bach, all done." Evelyn said. She picked up the now full basket off the counter. "Duw, my giddy aunt, heavy that is!" And putting both arms through the basket's handle she made to leave.

Agnes's raised voice filled the shop. " Where are you going, Evelyn? Aren't you going to pay the man? He doesn't run a charity shop mind. Talking food out of his mouth you are girl."

 Although her voice was raised, Agnes's smiling eyes gave her teasing game away.

"Yes...of course I am going to pay...I...I...was just about to get my purse out of the basket!" Evelyn stammered, obviously a little taken aback. "And how are you going to do that with both arms through the basket handle? Twp you are girl." Seeing her elder sisters cheeks reddening was too much for Agnes and she burst into laughter.

" Oh, you ...you...." Evelyn couldn't finish as she too burst out laughing. As did I and the nosey man who had stopped his snooping.

"What do we owe you, Rees?" Agnes eventually asked.

"All told it comes to one and six, ladies"

Agnes handed me the exact change and the two ladies left the shop, still badgering one another as they did so.

"They're a pair aren't they." Nosey man said. "Sorry, I had better introduce myself. My name is Brian, Brian Edwards." He politely held out his hand. "Rees, Rees Llewellyn." I said as I shook his hand.

" You may have noticed me looking around Mr Llewellyn. I noticed the for sale sign and came in to inspect the shop. I hope you don't mind."

"No, of course not. You wish to become a shop keeper?" I enquired.

"I already am Mr Llewellyn..." "Please, call me Rees." I interrupted. "Thank you, as I was saying, I have a shop up in Pontardawe, Rees. Not as big as this but it serves me well. My wife's expecting you see, so we need a bigger place to live. There's only two rooms in the living quarters in the Ponty shop and that wont be enough when the little one arrives."

"I see. Well, there are three rooms downstairs. The shop obviously, there's a middle room which I use as a store room and a back room which is the kitchen."

"Upstairs there are four rooms, not overly large but not small either. Would you like me to show you around?"

"That would be great, Rees, thank you."

As he had already inspected the shop I took him through to the middle room. It was full of boxes of all shapes and sizes, each packed with various items, bags of flour, jars of sweets, packets of tea. All the items that you would associate with a corner shop. The boxes of candles were piled from floor to ceiling. I sold a lot of candles. Most of the houses in the area did not have gas lamps.

As we entered the kitchen I heard him gasp. "what's up?" I asked. "The stove, Rees, I love that stove. My wife will love it too. All we have is a small stove, only room for a kettle and one cooking pot on the bloody thing. That stove will make all the difference."

To me it was just a stove, although it was rather large. The fire box was in the middle, open topped but with swing grids that could be pushed over the fire. Four in all.

To either side of the fire were ovens. One quite large, a roasting oven, the other smaller, a pudding oven. I only lit it in winter for a bit of warmth. I very rarely cooked on the grids and never used the ovens. I got most of my meals from the cafe over the road. I didn't see much point in cooking for one.

My grandfather used it to bake his famous Swansea pies. I could picture him now rolling out the pastry on the large table that still stood beneath the window. Cutting the pastry to fit the baking tin moulds. Once he was satisfied that the fit was good he would ladle out the filling from the large pot simmering on the stove. When all the pies were filled he would place the pastry caps on top of them and put them in the larger of the ovens.

He always sold out of pies by midday. Very popular they were. They cost threepence ha'penny each. The working men used to buy most of them on the way back from the night shift. Grab a pie then go for a pint. That was until a large bakery opened up at the top end of town. It produced a lot of pies and charged a ha'penny less. To many people a ha'penny saving meant a lot. Grandfather couldn't compete against such competition and stopped making his pies.

"Rees........Rees." Brian said quietly.

"Oh, sorry, Brian. Lost in thought I was then." I smiled apologetically.

I took him upstairs. He surveyed each of the four rooms, nodding his head in satisfaction as he looked around. He liked the view from the front room windows as you could see up Clase road. The higher up the road you looked the more affluent it became.

Many of the managers of the various industries in the lower valley had houses up on the higher parts of Clase Road. Away from the grubbiness of the town, away from the toxic smoke and where green grass and a few trees could grow.

I wondered if John Kelly lived up there. It suddenly struck me that I didn't know where he lived!

After the tour Brian was rather excited. "It's perfect, Rees. I know that my wife will love it, especially that stove. What's your asking price?"

"I'm selling it as a whole, that is business and building, including any stock you may wish to purchase for start up, until you can get your own of course. I've had a valuer in to look at the building and the books have been inspected by an accountant appointed by my solicitor. I'm asking for seventy five pounds plus any stock you may want."

"Seventy five pounds, that's quite a bit of money, Rees. I lease the Ponty shop, I don't own it. I have got some money saved and family will help out I'm sure. Right then, all being well with my solicitor once the books are checked and a valuer of my solicitors choice inspects the building, we have a deal."

"Excellent, Brian. You won't be sorry. This is a very busy shop most of the time. Yes, there are the odd days when trade is slow especially on Fridays. All down the market then, see what they can get on the cheap." I smiled as I said that.

"I need your solicitors name and address, Rees."

"Of course, just a minute." I wrote down the details, using my trusty pencil which I had removed from my apron pocket for the purpose, onto some note paper and handed to him.

"Well, I'll be off then, I can't wait to tell my wife. She will be so excited."

"One thing before you go, Brian. I will probably have left for London before the sale goes through. I hope that dealing solely with my solicitor wont be a problem?"

"No, I don't see as it will, Rees. Mostly solicitors involved anyway, not us ordinary folk."

I shook his hand as I said goodbye and wished him well.

The following morning, although the for sale sign was still up, I placed a closing down notice in the large shop window. If the sale fell through I would still leave and place the shop sale in the hands of my solicitor. The last day of trading would be the Saturday of next weekend, one week from today.

Life carried on much the same during that last week. Many of my customers telling me how sad it is that I am leaving, although they had known for some time that I was. Perhaps they thought that I wouldn't go. Thankfully, Copperopolis did not kill any more men in that last week.

Where was John Kelly? I thought he would have popped in with a copy of the contract and to say goodbye. Not to worry he did say that he was away a lot on business.

The last day of my life as a Morriston shop keeper quickly dawned. Customers were queuing at the door, not only to buy but also to wish me well in my new endeavour. Old Nelly came in, she looked so sad, her eyes studying the floor.

" I don't know what I'll do without you" she said in a faltering voice. I took her little basket off her and filled it with bread, bacon, sausage, eggs and a few other items that I forget now.

Opening the till I reached in my hand and took out a ten shilling note. I walked out from behind the counter and handed Nelly her now full basket. She made to pay me but I refused. Grabbing her hand I placed the note in her palm and gently closed her fingers over it.

Nelly looked at her hand in wonder and opened her fingers. Her face crumpled and the tears streamed down her cheeks. "Bless you, carriad, bless you."

She grabbed me tightly, nearly spilling the contents of her basket onto the floor. Her body racked with sobs of what I hoped were happiness. She released me and looked deeply into my eyes.

"You are a good man Mr Llewellyn, God bless you." Without looking back she exited the shop and was gone. A terrible feeling of sadness overcame me as I realised that I would never see old Nelly again.

I helped a lot of my less fortunate customers in the same way. Baskets heaped with food I refused to charge for and the odd few coins here and there. There was one special person that I had to see before the removal company came to pack up my stock and furniture for transportation to my new premises in London.

At 5.30pm the Reverend Harris arrived with a small army of helpers. I had made an arrangement with him where all my unsold perishable goods would be donated to the poor.

" This will be a great help, Rees. You would be surprised at the number of homeless people there are in the area. You know how it is, Rees, husband dies or is killed, that happens a lot around here, rent can't be paid and out on to the streets you go."

"Yes, Reverend, my own father was killed if you recall. My grandfather took me in or I'd have been in the workhouse for certain."

" You are one of the fortunate ones, Rees, for many it is either the workhouse or the streets. Anyway, what can we take from you?"

"All the bread, the eggs, the milk, the cheese, the bacon, the sausages. All of it can go."

 "Oh, and all of the vegetables on the display shelves." I added.

The little army, mostly of the younger church members, soon had all of the produce carefully packed up and carted off.

"I can't thank you enough, Rees. All of this will be distributed to the homeless shelters tonight. At least some of the poor buggers can enjoy some bread and cheese or sausage and egg or maybe even both."

The Reverend smiled and took my hand in both of his.

"Bless you, Rees. You are good man, I've heard that said by more than one person and more than once. I know you are busy so I'll be on my way. Good luck, Rees, come back and see us sometime."

After the Reverend and his little army had left I locked up the shop and made my way to little Timmy's house. It was a five minute walk up Woodfield Street. I turned left at the top of the street and into Morfydd Street.

I marvelled at St David's Church, which stood in the middle of the road. It was another cross roads but the church had been built in the middle, forcing the many horse drawn carts to manouver around it. I arrived at Timmy's house in Market Street, a small cottage to the left of the Libanus Chapel. I knocked the on the old door which had seen better days. The paint peeling off in many places, I couldn't make out what colour it was. Too much dirt and grime covered it, a result of exposure to the toxic smoke of the chimneys that surrounded the area.

Timmy's mother opened the door, she smiled when she recognised me. She was a very attractive woman with long mahogany coloured hair that swayed around her waist. Her eyes were of the most striking blue and her complexion as pale as a peach. Had she not been taken I may have tried to woo her myself.

"Hello Mr Llewellyn, what brings you here?" she asked in her strong Irish brogue.

"Is little Timmy about? I have something for him." She looked at me, her face full of compassion. "Come on in, I'll call him." I entered the tiny passageway and was motioned into a small but very well presented front room, it smelled of bee's wax. The surfaces of the wooden furniture shone.

At the call of his name I heard the thumping of feet on creaky stairs and Timmy bounded into the room.

"Hello Mr Llewellyn, what are you doing here?" he innocently asked. I didn't know if Timmy fully understood that I was leaving and wouldn't be back so I explained it to him. Poor little lad was very upset. He said that I was his friend, his grup friend. What did grup mean? I looked to his mother for help.

"Grup, Mr Llewellyn, is what Timmy calls grown ups."

Ah, the logic of a child. I could smell food cooking and realised that I was interrupting the dinner preparations. From within the folds of my over coat I produced a large jar of Timmy's favourite boiled sweets. His little face was a picture of joy. I said my goodbyes to mother and child and with a heavy heart made my way back to the shop to await the arrival of the removal company.

The stock that the would be owner, Mr Edwards, had agreed to purchase off me was neatly stored in the middle room. I met him for the second time when he came to the shop with his wife and his agent. His wife is the most delightful woman, in her 20's I would say and such a sweet face. Long curly shoulder length blond hair and emerald green eyes. And it was very evident that she was expecting.

"Oh, Mr Llewellyn, this shop is perfect. The stove, Brian told me it was a beauty but...oh...I shall have so much fun cooking on it."

The way her face lit up with delight would have melted even the coldest of hearts.

Before they left I advised Brian that I would definitely be in London when the contracts were due to be exchanged but that my solicitor had my authority to act on my behalf.

I was regretting my haste with the London shop. I should have gone through the proper legal channels. Of course that was not mentioned to my solicitor. I told him that I was tired of the shop and wished to travel for a while.

I hadn't seen John Kelly since our business was concluded. Perhaps he will come tomorrow before I leave for London. He had promised to get me a copy of the contract. If he was away on business then there wasn't much that could be done about it. He had been a customer of my grandfather for years. Long before I started working in the shop. However, my grandfather did treat him with a coldness, I now recall. Although John always had that familiar smile on his face despite this. I assumed that it was my grandfather. He was like that with some people, not many, but the odd few.

I heard rather than saw the wagons as they approached. I stepped outside to the sight of two huge wagons, each pulled by a team of four horses, thundering down lower Woodfield Street. It was a truly magnificent sight. The wagons had emblazoned on their sides the name of the removal company: Pickfords. They pulled up outside of the shop. The respective drivers placed a nose bag over the heads of their horses. The bags filled with grain to keep the horses quiet whilst the work progressed. The drivers stayed with the horses and the other four men came into the shop.

"Where do you want us to start, mate?" the older man asked.

"All this is ready to go." I said, pointing to the packed crates. John Kelly's make shift seat was hoisted up by one of the men and taken out to the wagon.

This was soon followed by other crates as the removal men busied themselves in the task at hand.

All my wordily goods disappeared into the wagons at an astonishing pace. It took a little over two hours to empty the shop, apart from the stock being left as agreed with Mr Edwards.

"That's it then, Mr Llewellyn, all is onboard. We'll transport it to High Street station. When the London train arrives we'll load your goods onto it."

"If I understand correctly, your counterparts in London will be waiting to unload my goods off the train and deliver them to my London address?"

"Yes, Mr Llewellyn, all is arranged. No need for you to worry about that. Now then, if you wouldn't mind signing on the dotted line and we'll be on our way." He indicated where I was to sign and handed me a copy of the note.

I gave each man a tanner, for which they were very thankful, and watched as the nose bags were removed from the horses. The drivers took their places on the wagons and with a flick of the reigns the horses moved forward, clop by clop, pulling the wagons along behind them. I watched as the wagons turned around and made their way back up Woodfield Street and towards Swansea.

After locking up the shop and checking that all was secure I made my way upstairs and into the second bedroom. Here, I had put up a makeshift cot for myself. Reaching beneath it I retrieved my strong box and placed it into a custom made bag, especially strengthened for the purpose. I quickly undressed, put on my night-shirt and got into my cot, hoping that sleep would come quickly as tomorrow was going to be a busy day. Solicitor first thing and then off to High street station and the train to London.

Morning dawned, cold and crisp. I looked out of the window, frost coated the pavements and the windows of the buildings opposite. Glinting in the feeble light of the gas lamp. Smoke bellowed from many of the houses chimneys adding to the already thickening smog.

Quickly, I washed and dressed, it was too cold to dally. My normal working attire of shirt, tie, trousers, boots and leather apron were swapped for a more formal but comfortable look. I wore a freshly laundered shirt, a nice blue tie and a grey, loose fitting three piece suit. Not an expensive one but it looked presentable. Grabbing the bag that contained my strong box I went downstairs. I looked around at the almost empty shop. Memories of my grandfather swirled through my mind. I could see him behind the counter, a short rotund man, with a bald head surrounded by a circle of very fine and over length white hair. Smiling brown eyes looking out of a full and slightly red face. I pictured him smiling and chatting with some customers and being a sour faced, grunting old ogre with those that he, for whatever reason, didn't seem to like. I missed him then, deeply and profoundly. I hoped he would understand my decision to leave.

Taking one last look around I opened the door and exited the shop. I was surprised that my hand trembled as I placed the key in the lock and turned it for the last time. All was quiet, the men were already at work and it was too early for other folk to be out and about. Making my way up Woodfield Street, I realised that I would not be seeing it again for some time, if ever.

By prior arrangement my solicitor had opened early so that I could conclude all my business dealings regarding the sale of the shop. I entered the solicitors office which was very well decorated. The walls were covered with a plush, deep red wallpaper. Brass gas lights with ornate glass covers adorned the wall facing me.

One on either side of a large gold framed picture which depicted a countryside hunting scene. A red jacketed rider sat atop a chestnut coloured horse as it jumped a fence in pursuit of the hounds that could be seen in the distance.

"Ah, Mr Llewellyn, please, do be seated."

The solicitor, Mr Abraham, was sat behind an impressive wooden desk that stood like an ornate sarcophagus in the room. The columns that made up its legs were carved to look like tree trunks, the leaf covered branches reaching out across the front and around the sides of the desk. The highly polished surface reflecting the yellow glow of the gas lamps. I sat in an equally impressive carved wooden chair, sinking in to its well padded seat.

"Firstly, I would like to wish you well in your travels. I do hope that you will return one day. Many of the Morriston folk will miss your acts of kindness. Word does get around you know."

I could feel the colour rising to my cheeks.

"Oh, I didn't do that much really. Just a little help here and there."

"I'm sure that is so, Mr Llewellyn" the solicitor, said.

"Now, to business. May I have the key to your premises please? I have all the paperwork in-order. I will need you to sign the deed of sale and a receipt to prove that I have received the key."

I duly handed over the key. Mr Abraham placed the deed of sale in front of me and handed me the quill. I signed the deed which was removed and then replaced with an identical document.

"That will be your copy." Mr Abraham explained.

I signed it and again it was quickly removed.

"Come in gentlemen." Mr Abraham called out.

The office door opened and two men entered. Both looked to be in their sixties. Each wore very fine navy serge three piece suits, matching navy ties and bright white, well starched collars. Gold cuff links held the shirt cuffs closed and each wore a gold tie pin. Their black shoes shone like polished marble. I felt very under dressed.

"These gentlemen are, Mr Meredith and, Mr Owen. Both are partners in legal practise up the hill in Llangyfellach. They will act as witnesses."

I nodded my head in understanding but did not speak. With the deed duly witnessed Mr Meredith and Mr Owen left the office. Not a word was spoken, it was all very business like.

"When Mr Edwards and his solicitor come to do their part of the transaction, I will pay the cheque made payable to Abraham & Co Solicitors for the sum of seventy seven pounds into the business account. The seventy seven pounds includes the purchase of your stock by Mr Edwards. It will take a few days to clear. Once it has I'll instruct the bank to wire the amount through to your London bank which is......ah, yes, Lloyd's in Cheap side, City of London. I will also hand the key over to Mr Edwards and conclude all business. I must stress that the sale will only be finalised upon clearance of Mr Edwards cheque, so don't worry yourself about that."

Mr Abraham stood up, I quickly did the same. He handed me my witnessed copy of the deed of sale. He held out his hand which I took in mine and we shook on the deal.

" It has been a pleasure doing business with you, Mr Llewellyn. How would you like to pay my fee, now or shall I remove the fee from the balance of the property purchase price?" He said as he handed me his bill.

I looked at the bill, all itemised very neatly. The price of each service duly written down. A little over 3 shillings in total, very reasonable.

"I'll settle the bill now Mr Abraham, then it's all done and dusted."

I reached down and retrieved my bag from beneath the ornate chair. Removing the strong box, I retrieved the key from my jacket pocket, where I had put it for ease of access, and fought to open the box but with a click it opened. I handed Mr Abraham the exact amount of money due him and in return he handed me a receipt. Before closing the strong box I placed a few pennies, a few shillings and other small change into my trouser pocket. It would be too troublesome having to open the strong box every time I needed some money. With a further 'goodbye' and a handshake I left the office and made my way to the cab rank. My train for London would depart in an hours time.

John Kelly didn't show his up as I'd hoped he would.

Having hailed a cab, I climbed in and instructed the driver to take me to High Street Station. With a flick of the reigns the horse pulled forward and we headed out of Morriston. The journey to Swansea was not pleasant.

The cab shook and shuddered over the cobbled road surface. In some parts the cobbles had become displaced and pot holes took their place, the cab went over one such pot hole, it was a bone jarring experience that I hoped would not be repeated. Travelling along Neath road through Plas Marl and down towards Havod brought you into the very heart of Copperopolis. To my left I could see the massive piles of coal in the numerous coal yards along the river bank. Small shunting engines meandering through the buildings like a lost troop of ants. Some laden with coal and some laden with copper ore, both the life blood of Copperopolis.

The smell was far stronger here, a sulphurous metallic essence that assaulted one's nostrils and filled one's mouth with a most obnoxious taste. How could men work in this devils playground? Many men did, thousands of them. It was dirty and dangerous work but it paid quite well. The only problem being that if you lasted 10 years in the poisonous environment then you were the exception rather than the rule. Many men did not live past the age of forty five.

The chimney stacks were numerous. All standing tall and proud whilst spewing out ominous amounts of black/grey smoke that had nowhere to go. It hung in the air like a giant cloud, waiting for the westerly winds to pick up and disperse it. The Neath canal was full of barges bringing coal from the numerous mines further up the valley into the coal yards. Others returning, carrying various other products, such as pottery produced by the pottery works on the banks of the river Tawe.

Over in the distance I could see Kilvey Hill, shrouded in a toxic mist. Bereft of vegetation, grass couldn't grow here only a few stunted shrubs dotted its surface.

Onward and into Landore, a built up area with rows of houses flowing up the hill side. Each a dwelling of those that worked in Copperopolis. The stones of which they were built stained a dirty brown by the ever present smoke. There were many corner shops here but there were more than enough customers for each shop. Even at this earlier hour there were people entering and leaving the shops as my cab trundled by.

Into Swansea's High Street and down towards the station we went. The cobbled road surface was of better quality here but I would be glad to get out of this cab. It was like a travelling through a different world, people milling about, some into the various shops that the High Street supported, some into the station and some just window shopping.

The cab pulled up outside the station. I gladly got out and reached up to pay the driver his fee. The horse shied a little and stamped a shod-den hoof on the cobbles. As soon as I moved away it quietened and, with a flick of the reigns, the driver sent them off in search of another customer. They hadn't gone more than a few feet before a rather portly gentleman held out his hand, a signal for the cab to stop, which it did. The portly gent managed to climb aboard, with some difficulty and the cab moved off.

The pleasure of walking cannot be over emphasized after that short but very unpleasant cab journey. I walked into the station and found the ticket office. The man behind the glass window didn't look at all happy. He looked as if he had found a penny but lost a pound.

"Ticket to London please. One way."

"You want first class, second class or the wooden seats?"

"What are the wooden seats?" I enquired.

"The cheap seats, duw, don't travel much do you!"

"No, I don't, never been further than Neath and then only once."

He looked at me as if I had grown an extra nose!

"I'll have the wooden seats then." I said puffing my chest out.

The unhappy ticket man grabbed a reel of tickets and pulled one ticket free.

"Two shillings that will be." He spat out.

I placed the money in the tray below the hole in the window. A hand appeared and quickly disappeared taking my money with it. It then re-appeared, dropped my ticket in the tray before disappearing again. Picking up the ticket I nodded at sour face behind the glass and made for the platform. The train was already waiting. A gently hissing iron monster.

I sat by the window on a very hard seat, placing my bag on the floor behind my lower legs. This was going to be a long and uncomfortable journey. I watched as the more affluent passengers climbed into the first and second class carriages. I could have travelled in the posh seats but why spend extra money when I didn't need to. It was obvious that most of those sat around me were working men and women. They were probably only taking a short journey, maybe to Morriston, Llansamlet or Neath.

With a shriek of a whistle the train gave a jerk and started to chuff away. Huge plumes of steam, smoke and ash engulfed the trailing carriages as the engine pulled forward. Once clear of the station the engine slowly picked up speed. The carriage gently swayed as the train made its way along the track. Soon it was travelling over the bridge that spanned the Neath canal. The bridge was designed by that clever fellow, Isambard Kingdom Brunel and built in 1850. It is a very impressive wooden structure it must be said.

The view from the bridge was equally impressive, or not, that would depend on the observer's opinion. Looking out over the heart of Necropolis, this huge industrial beast. Its limbs, the numerous stone built buildings that meandered for miles along the banks of the river Tawe. Its lungs, those tall smoking chimneys belching out thick acrid black smoke as the beast breathed. Its veins, the numerous railway tracks that flowed throughout its sprawling mass. Delivering the materials that gave it life.

You would have to see it to understand the huge scale of the industry that filled my view out of the grimy carriage window. I settled back and made myself as comfortable as possible, which was not that easy. Pulling my lower legs back, my calf's tightly gripped my bag. I must have nodded off as I was awoken by a tugging sensation in my lower legs. Opening my eyes I saw a very dirty flat cap, atop an equally dirty jacketed pair of shoulders as the would be thief attempted to steal my bag.

I moved my legs a little forward and released the bag. As the thief started to rise I smashed my elbow into his face, hearing a crunch I knew that his nose had broken. The thief staggered backwards, both hands covering his shattered nose.

" GET OUT OF MY SIGHT!" I shouted.

He very quickly scrambled away and was soon lost among the other passengers. Many pairs of eyes were upon me, I was very concious of that.

"You should call the guard, mate. Bloody robbing bastard!" said a tired looking man. His face and clothes blackened by coal dust. One of the area's many coal miners.

"No, let it be. He got a broken nose for his trouble."

I re- took my seat, placing my bag firmly behind my legs. What a good start to my new life! I expected the thief to return with a few accomplices, thankfully, he didn't. No sleep for the rest of the journey, once bitten, twice shy as they say. As the train made its designated stops along the route, the carriage slowly emptied. Once we had past Neath there were only a few people remaining.

The hours slowly passed, I entertained myself by looking at the changing scenery as the train steamed along. Fields with sheep busy eating the grass. Fields with Cows doing the same. Then the train would pass through a heavily wooded area which caused a premature dusk as the light was obscured by tree trunks sporting leafless, skeleton branches. The train crossed over many bridges that afforded many varied views.

It was starting to get dark as the train steamed through more and more built up areas. London can't be far now. The roads that I could see through the grimy window were filled with horse drawn carts of varying sizes. Each laden with goods of all descriptions, hay, meat, potatoes, cloth and one piled high with wooden barrels.

During the long journey I was struck by how much of the countryside had given way to the industrial beast. Green fields lost to the sprawl of factory buildings and smoking chimney stacks. Where will it all end I wondered. Would the fields of grass consumed by the Sheep and the Cows, themselves be consumed by the infernal factory buildings of industry?

LONDON.

It was dark when the train eventually came to a stop in Paddington station. Steam hissed out of the engines release valves and it disappeared into a billowing white cloud. I reached down grabbed my bag and stood up. Having taken only a few steps down the aisle towards the door I was violently pushed from behind causing me to stumble but not fall. My assailant jumped on my back trying to force me to the floor. His arm wrapped tightly around my neck trying to choke me. I am a strong man, years of lifting heavy sacks of flour and sugar had seen to that. Reaching over my head I grabbed a handful of greasy hair. Quickly bending forward, pulling my assailant by the hair as I did so caused him to lose his grip. He rolled off my back and landed with a thump on the floor.

"You!" I exclaimed. It was the unsuccessful bag thief who had failed once again. I aimed a punch at his already ruined nose and let it fly. He cried out in pain as his nose erupted in a shower of blood.

Grabbing him tightly by the collar I half dragged, half carried him off the train. People stared at the sight of us, me striding forward like a bull dragging this bloody faced man behind me. I saw a police constable standing further along the platform and headed straight for him.

"Good evening, officer. This man has twice tried to steal my bag. Once as we left Swansea and just now as I went to get off the train. I'm afraid he was injured in his attempts." I smiled a 'you know what I mean' smile.

"Not again, Albert! Will you ever learn?"

"You know this man, officer?"

"I'm afraid so. Albert, likes to ride trains. Likes to rob the people on them too. Never known him to attack people though."

" But he got on the train in Swansea. That's bloody miles away."

"Yes, Mr.........?" "Llewellyn, Rees Llewellyn" I quickly answered.

"That's what Albert does. Travels the railways all over the country. Stealing as he goes. He gets caught, gets banged up for a while. Gets released and starts again."

Turning to the bloodied Albert the officer asked. "Why attack Mr Llewellyn, you've never been violent before?"

"Coz he broke my bleedin' nose!" Albert exclaimed.

"Bleeding is right." the officer laughingly said. Albert scowled at him but then whimpered in pain as his broken nose protested.

"I'll need a statement off you Mr Llewellyn." he said producing his note book.

I gave him my statement in detail including my London address and made to leave.

" Cable Street, Spitalfields. Is that correct Mr Llewellyn?"

"Yes, officer. I have taken over a shop there. Why do you ask?"

"No particular reason. But you be careful and keep your wits about you. Spitalfields is not a place for the un-wary"

I was about to ask why but he had grabbed Albert and was already walking off at a brisk pace, pulling the reluctant thief behind him. What the hell did he mean by that? John had told me that Spitalfields was a respectable, affluent part of London. The seeds of doubt began to slowly grow in my mind.

And so, on the 15th of April 1885 my life in London got off to a shaky start. I left the station and quickly found a Cab. Actually, I had my pick of cabs as there were a number of them lined up outside the station. I chose a cab that had a wonderful black stallion in front.

"Cable Street, Spitalfields. Please driver."

"Cable Street, Spitalfields? Sorry guv, I don't go into Spitalfields."

"Why ever not, is my money not good enough?"

"It's not that, I only do the 'ospitals and the west end addresses. You need the scratch cabs further down the line."

I wished the driver a good evening and walked down the line to where the scratch cabs stood. The difference was immediately apparent, these cabs looked a little worse for wear and were not very clean. Before getting in to the cleanest cab I could find I gave the driver my destination.

"Right you are, Boss. Get in."

Sitting down on the not so clean seat I placed my bag at my side. The cab stank! Worse than the chimney smoke of Copperopolis! The cab lurched this way and that as the driver negotiated his way around other cabs and various obstacles that hindered his progress. I was bounced around the cab like a Jack in the box on its spring! I grabbed my bag before it got bounced out of the window. It made the Morriston to Swansea journey seem like luxury. The further away from the station we travelled the darker the streets became. The gas lamps becoming fewer, the streets narrower, dirtier and smellier. What the hell had I let myself in for?

After a journey of around twenty minutes, through some of the dirtiest streets imaginable, we arrived at, 124 Cable Street. I paid the driver, who wasted no time in leaving! Standing on the pavement I looked at the shop. Even in the very poor light I could see how run down it was. It was also boarded up. Although a large, new looking padlock secured the door. A voice in the darkness called out.

 "Mr Llewellyn. Are you Mr Llewellyn?" Out of the gloom a small figure appeared. A boy of around ten years of age, dressed in rags and very dirty.

"Yes, I am Mr Llewellyn. Who wants to know?"

"Mr McCarthy, he told me to wait until you showed up. Gave me this to give to you." He handed me a new looking key, which I presumed belonged to the new looking padlock.

"And where is Mr McCarthy? I'd like a few words with him."

"I dunno where he is. All I knows is that he asked me to wait for you and give you the key."

"How long have you been waiting, boy?" I asked.

"Hours mister, bleedin' freezin' I am. These clothes don't keep out the cold."

Despite my anger and despair I couldn't help but feel sorry for the poor mite.

"Have you eaten, boy?"

"No, mister. And my name is Michael."

"I haven't eaten for hours myself. Is there a food shop or something near, Michael?"

"There's a jacket potato seller in the next street. Does lovely grub he does. When I gots some money I always gets me a hot potato. I don't gets it that often though." Michael said rather sadly.

"Right then, Michael, jacket potato it is. Lead on."

We walked the short distance to the next street. I have never encountered such filth in all my life. Horse shit covered the streets and had splattered onto the pavements in many places. The smell was terrible. A mixture of horse and human excrement, along with rotting vegetables, urine and god knows what else. It made Morriston smell positively fragrant. The potato seller had his stall in one of the few cleaner spots in the street. The glow of the oven clearly visible in the poor light. The oven was on wheels and attached to the front was a long handle by which the seller pulled it along.

"What's it to be guv'nor ?" the potato seller asked. He didn't even glance at Michael. He probably assumed, quite rightly, that he didn't have any money.

" Two hot potato's please, with some butter if you have it."

"Ah, don't have no butter but I got some cheese."

"That will do, cheese it is."

The seller handed the potato's to me. Each supported on a large wad of newspaper so as I didn't burn my hands. They had already been cut down the middle, the cheese melting into the potato. I paid the fourpence and handed Michael his potato. Even though it was steaming hot, it disappeared in seconds. The only visible signs of discomfort were his slightly watering eyes. The poor mite was starving! He watched as I slowly ate mine, blowing on it all the while to cool it down.

"Still hungry?" I asked him.

" Always hungry, mister. Sometimes I donts eat for a few days. Depends if I earns any money see. Also if I manages to keep it. Too many thief's around here."

Bloody hell, what is this place that allows its children to starve? Morriston had its homeless, its people of the streets. It also had a lot of shelters to care for them. And a community spirit that came together in times of need.

"Another potato, please." I called out to the seller.

Michael devoured that one in seconds also.

"Thanks, mister. I aint hungry no more."

"Glad to hear it. Well, I'd better get back and see to the shop. Will you be alright? Here's threepence, you've earned that."

"Thanks, but I can't take it. I knows that I'll get it nicked off me." Michael looked at the floor as he talked.

"Tell you what, call in the shop tomorrow and I'll see what I can do to help you out."

"Thanks, mister. I'll do that." and he started to walk off.

"Michael." I called out. He turned to look at me.

"My name is Rees."

Michael smiled, gave a wave and disappeared into the gloom. Picking up my bag I headed back to the shop. Feeling extremely daunted by the thought of what was inside. Full of trepidation I placed the key in to the padlock and turned it. The lock gave a soft click and opened. Removing the padlock from its bracket and turning the handle the door opened. Its hinges squeaking in protest. I stepped inside the shop. The light from the gas lamp across the street pushed feebly into the darkness. I could just about see the long counter that stretched off and disappeared into inky blackness.

On the wall behind the counter was a gas lamp and atop the counter was a box of matches! I picked up the box, pushed out the little drawer and took out a match. Lifting up the hinged flap and opening the small door set into the counter I moved behind it.

I turned the gas knob on the lamp and was greeted by a gentle hissing sound. It was working! I quickly struck the match which erupted into a yellow flame and lit the lamp. Slowly turning up the gas until the flame burned brightly. As the darkness retreated more lamps appeared, four in all. Soon the shop was ablaze with light. To my amazement I saw that the shop was big, very big. Closing and locking the front door, the key was on the inside for some reason, I looked around.

The counter ran the whole length of the shop, it must be about thirty five to forty foot long. Behind it were row upon row of shelving. The distance from the counter to the front of the shop must have been at least another thirty foot or more. Four iron columns, evenly spaced supported the floor above. They were painted black and had a ribbed design running from floor to ceiling. Where they met the ceiling they had what looked like a bunch of grapes design. Very ornate indeed. I hadn't imagined or expected this. From the outside, due to the boarded up windows, it didn't look so big.

Moving behind the counter I entered the passageway that led to the rooms behind. There were two rooms, one to the right and one to the left. A little further down and set to the left was the stairway to the upstairs. To the right of the stairs was a door set into the rear wall. That was obviously the back door. I went in to the room to my left. Lighting the gas lamp on the wall just inside of the door, I could see that all of the contents of my Morriston shop and home seemed to be in here. Neatly stacked and to my surprise, the shop stock and my personal effects had been separated. One side of the room filled with the shop stock and the other with my effects. This room was also very large. I turned the lamp down, stepped out into the passage and entered the other room.

Lighting the lamp I could see that this room was also very large. An enormous cooking range dominated one side, all black leaded and looking quite smart. All the upstairs rooms were also quite large. Perhaps my earlier fears were unfounded after all. This place had great potential. Returning to the room where my effects were stored I rummaged through them looking for the folding cot which was the partner of the one I'd left in Morriston. Turning up the lamp to see better I soon found it. Adding a sheet and a couple of blankets my bed was done. Lighting a candle I went back into the shop and turned off the gas lamps, made sure the door was securely locked and went back into my 'bedroom'. I turned off the lamp and secured the candle on top of a packing crate. I didn't bother to undress, I was exhausted by the journey and the mental anguish. Blowing out the candle, I lay down on the cot and was instantly asleep.

I was awakened by clattering and banging sounds. What the hell was going on? Jumping up off the cot I quickly made my way to the shop area. The boards were being removed from the windows letting in the natural light and also showing me that the windows will need a good clean. I watched as the boards were loaded onto a hand cart. One man removing the boards and another loading them. Both looked to be in their mid 20's and both wore what could only be described as work uniforms. Very dirty ones at that. Greasy, dirty flat caps, no shirt collar visible on either. Both of them wore jackets that may have once been grey but were now more a sooty black. The elbows holed and the cuffs fraying. Both men wore dirty brown leather aprons.

Opening the front door I stepped out outside.

"Bore Da" I called out.

The men looked at me, then at each other, shrugged their shoulders and carried on with the task in hand.

I'd forgotten that I wasn't in Morriston!

"Sorry, Good Morning." I said

"Mornin' Boss." One answered. "We'll be finished soon. Just these last few boards to take down."

"That's alright, no problem. Have you seen Jack McCarthy this morning?" I asked.

"Not this mornin', no. Saw him early yesterday. Told us to come and take the boards down today." He carried on working as he answered.

"Did he mention anything about coming here himself? I need to talk to him."

"Not to me he didn't. He mention anything to you, Tom?" He asked his mate.

"Nah, not a bleedin' thing." Came the disinterested reply.

The last board was taken down and loaded onto the hand cart.

"That's us done then. Going back to the yard now. If I see Jack on the way I'll tell him you want to see him."

I fished about in my trouser pocket gave each man a few pennies. After thanking me profusely the very grateful duo went on their way. The wheels of the cart rattling on the cobblestones. Returning inside, my bladder reminded me that I needed to use the toilet badly.

Opening the back door I saw the out house at the rear of the rather small yard. Brick built and with a slate roof! The one in Morriston was made of wood. My situation didn't appear to be as dire as I had thought. As I opened the out house door, the smell nearly knocked me off my feet! I stumbled backwards, gagging and coughing. Hell, I couldn't use that, not a chance. I recovered my composure. What to do? Somewhere close by a window opened and I looked up at the adjoining house. A chamber pot appeared out of the open window followed by the hand that was holding it. The pot was turned upside down and its contents splattered onto the surface of the yard next door! I stared in disbelief as the pot disappeared inside and the window shut. Now I knew one of the reasons why this place stank to high heaven.

Returning to my makeshift bedroom come storeroom, I rummaged through the stock until I found what I was looking for, bottles of bleach and a long handled scrubbing brush. I took my handkerchief out of my pocket and suitably armed returned to the outhouse. With my handkerchief held firmly over my nose I began to clean. It took me about half an hour of gagging and dry heaving before the toilet was clean. I used two bottles of bleach and cleaned every surface inside that little room. The smell was gone and the toilet usable. Thankfully, the flush worked.

I went back inside and coming out of the passageway into the shop I saw a rather large man leaning on the counter. A battered hat sat on his head, looked to be what may have been in bowler in its former life. He wore a red neckerchief tied in knot in the front. And a salt and pepper coloured jacket. I couldn't see the rest of him because of the counter. He looked up as he saw me enter. His face was clean shaven but horribly pock marked. A small pox survivor I thought. He had small dark eyes, set either side of a big bulbous nose. A drinker as-well no doubt. I guessed he was about fifty or maybe sixty, with that mashed up face it was hard to tell.

"You must be, Mr Llewellyn."

"Who wants to know?" I asked.

"My name is Jack McCarthy." He answered, holding out a huge hand.

"I'm glad you turned up." I said, shaking that huge paw as I did so.

"I hope you have the contract with you." I asked, smiling my best smile. I didn't want to get on the wrong end of this man.

"Contract?....What contract?" Jack asked, a puzzled look on his face.

"The one that you sent to John Kelly, the one that I wasn't given a copy of."

Jack visibly deflated before my eyes, his face a picture of disbelief.

"I don't fuckin' believe this! Don't tell me that after all these years that fuckin' runt is at it again!"

"What do you mean?" The panic in my voice clearly audible.

"I'll be right back...er......Rees, is it? I need a beer!"

"Wait, Jack!" Too late. He was out of the door and storming off up the street. What the hell was going on?

He returned some minutes later carrying a large crate full of beer bottles. I'm not a drinking man normally, I do enjoy the odd pint or two but not very often. I think today might be an exception!

"Have you got any chairs, Rees? We maybe here for some time!"

"Er.....y....yes." I stammered.

I went to get the chairs and on my return found an open beer waiting for me on the counter. I gave a chair to Jack and took my place at the bar. We sat facing each other.

Jack took a long pull at his beer before talking.

"There is no contract, Rees. There never was a contract."

"But, John said, he sa......"

"Shut up and listen!" Jack said, his voice a growl.

"John wrote to me out of the blue. I hadn't heard from that bastard in years! He told me about you, how good a man you were and that you needed a bit of help to find a shop in London."

I listened intently but I didn't like what I was hearing.

"I owed him a favour, one that I was loathe to return. I'd got myself in a bit of money trouble many years back. It was all his bloody fault anyway but I'll get to that later. As much as I hated it, John bailed me out."

He took another long pull on his beer.

"I told him I had this empty shop and that you could lease. I've had it for a while now but haven't been able to lease it, too big for many people. Not suitable for a doss house either. All the internal walls would have to be taken out see, Rees."

It was my turn to take a long pull on my beer. It tasted very bitter, the Welsh beer is much better.

"I told him that all you had to do was turn up and it was yours to lease. Simple as that, no bloody contract involved"

"You mean......"

"Yes, Rees, you've been conned, we've both been had. John The Con strikes again!"

I took a huge swig of beer, nearly choking myself as I did so. When I'd finished coughing and spluttering I explained more.

"But that can't be right. John gave me a large envelope with all the official documents in. He said that you knew people and that's how it was done so quickly. I had to pay him ten pounds to cover the costs!"

Jack spat out a mouthful of beer on hearing that. It splattered over the surface of the counter.

"I don't fuckin' believe it! That little shit! The fuckin' bastard!"

" For fucks sake, Jack, what's going on?" I rarely swore but I could have sworn for the whole of Wales at that moment!

Jack reached down into the crate at his feet and pulled out another bottle, popping the top he took a large swig.

"Better get yourself another beer too, Rees, this will take some explaining."

I listened in disbelief at the story Jack was telling me.

John Kelly was born in Spitalfields, as was Jack. They both went to the same schools. Both grew up in fairly comfortable surroundings, not all of Spitalfields was as poor as this area. They played together, were the best of friends and always did things together. They both started work on the same day at the Iron Works on the banks of the river Thames. Jack as a manual labourer, his academic skill not as good as John, who worked in the accounts office. John soon learned accountancy skills and was doing very well for himself. There was a problem however, and that was that John liked to gamble. Cards to be exact but he was not a good card player and it wasn't long before he owed a lot of money to the wrong people. He was in deep and didn't know how to get himself out.

"He borrowed money to pay his gambling debts. The people he borrowed the money off, Rees, were not men you messed with. Cut your throat as good as look at you. When he couldn't repay the money, with interest added, things got ugly."

Jack went on to tell me how these men arranged for John to be taught how to forge documents and signatures. They knew he had a responsible job and handled the finances at the iron works. It took many months of schooling but eventually he became an expert document forger. Only the most experienced eye would be able to tell the difference between the real deal and the forgery. It was worth the investment. To them, John was a gold mine.

"In all fairness to John, he didn't have a choice. They would have killed him. Have no doubt about that."

"He shouldn't have got himself into such a fucking mess." I reasoned.

"Easy to judge, Rees. You don't have a fuckin' clue how it works, do you?"

Truth was I didn't. This was a whole new world to me!

Jack told me how John had started to falsify the accounts at the iron works. Taking money out of the safe, money he was entrusted to look after. How he also forged the signature on the company cheques and cashed them himself. Not large amounts, a few pounds here and a few pounds there.

"He did it for months, Rees. And because no one had noticed he got too bold. He couldn't catch up with the debt because of the interest being added each day. It was a no win situation. He got desperate and started cashing cheques for much larger amounts."

Jack explained that one day, John was in the bank cashing a forged cheque. As the bank clerk handed him the money, ten pounds this time, a police officer grabbed him.

"I don't know why but he wasn't prosecuted, Rees. It seems that the owner of the iron works didn't want it known that he had been so easily swindled."

"So what happened next?" I anxiously asked.

"John came to me one day and said that he was going away. To a place where he could put all this behind him and start again."

Jack finished his beer and reached for another one. I was too stunned at his story to drink much of mine.

"And that's what he did, he disappeared for years, Nobody knew where he'd gone. Until now that is."

"But didn't you say that you owed him a favour. He got you out of some trouble?"

"Yes, years ago now, he turned up in Spitalfields. He walked into my shop in Dorset Street as cool as you like. See, Rees, I was sacked at the same time he was. Seems I was judged because we were mates, the fucker! That's why I started up the shop, I answer to no one but myself now!"

He went silent for a moment and then continued.

"Jack! How are you? Long time no see." The bastard said to me.

By the look on Jack's face I could see that the memory was not a pleasant one.

"And didn't he look the toff! All collar and cuffs he was. Smart stove pipe hat, cutaway jacket, silk waist coat, pressed grey trousers and shit covered shoes. At least Spitalfields welcomed him home!"

"I take it then that you weren't pleased to see him?"

"No, Rees, I fuckin' wasn't!"

Jack explained how John's crimes had affected his mother. She was a broken woman. How could her precious son be such a bastard, not only a gambler but a thief too boot.

"Her health failed her, Rees. I spent pounds on doctors to try and see her right. Like an Aunty to me she was. And where was her loving son?

Jacks face grew red with anger. His beer finished he fished out another, popped the top and took a few mouthfuls. Some of the beer dribbled down his chin and dripped off the end. Wiping his mouth and chin with a dirty sleeve, he continued the story.

"When she died I paid for the funeral and all that goes with it. I made sure she had a good send off. I was all she had, Rees. Her husband had died years ago and John was the only child."

He raised the bottle to his lips and emptied it with a few huge gulps.

"So when I sees him standing in my shop I wanted to punch his fuckin' lights out! Only I couldn't, well not straight away, I needed his help. With the doctors fees and the funeral costs I was in debt myself."

"So, you had to ask him for money?" I pensively asked.

"YES, I FUCKIN' DID!" Jack yelled.

I nearly fell off my chair, I wasn't expecting that.

In a calmer voice Jack continued.

"I told him about his mother. How he had destroyed her. The doctors, the funeral and what it had cost me."

Another large swig of beer. The bottle slammed down on to the counter!

"That smug bastard just smiled. Blame me for it do you? The fucker asked me! Then he takes out this small red leather case from his jacket inside pocket. Opens it, counts out a few notes and drops them on the floor!"

He raised the bottle to his lips once again, it was empty. Reaching down into the crate he got another one.

"That should cover it he said. Well, if he did, I flew at him, pushed him through the shop door and landed a punch that sent him sprawling into the shit covered road."

He started to laugh. The beer was taking effect.

"Anyway, he picks himself up, covered in shit he is. What good his posh clothes now. And to top it off his hat got crushed by a cart! He stormed off and I never saw him again."

It was my turn to take a few swigs of beer.

"That must be the reason why I'd never seen him wearing a hat." I mused.

"What!" Jack exclaimed, looking at me as if I were an idiot.

"Sorry, Jack. Then he writes you out of the blue and you help him?"

"It was over twenty years ago, Rees. I thought forgive and forget. We were good friends once. I honestly thought that he was trying to do you a favour. Big fuckin' mistake that was. Because now I've helped him to rip you off."

I rubbed a hand over my face trying to get my head around what Jack had told me.

"I don't understand, Jack. John was a customer of my grandfather and myself for many years. I never heard anyone say a bad word about him nor did I hear him say a bad word about anyone either. He was a well liked member of the community."

"That maybe so, but a Leopard doesn't change its spots. John is up to his old tricks again. I wonder who he owes money to this time?"

"I need to report this to the police, Jack."

"And how are you going to prove it, Rees? Got a copy of the contract have you? Got a receipt for the ten pounds have you? You got shit, Rees. How could you be so fuckin' stupid!"

"I told you, Jack. I've known him for years. I had no reason not to trust him. Yes, I did question it in my head but convinced myself that John was a good friend and that it would be alright."

"So, what will you do now that you know the truth, go back to Morriston?" Jack asked.

"I should go back and tackle that bastard but I have a feeling that he will be long gone. My shop is sold, well almost. I can't let the buyers down. Lovely couple they are. No, there's only one thing for it. I have to make a go of it here."

I finished my beer and got myself another. Jack did the same. Clinking the bottles together in a mock toast to our mutual despair, we took a few mouthfuls. I definitely prefer Welsh beer!

"I'll send a few of my lads around later to help you get set up. That is the least I can do."

"Thank You, I'd appreciate that."

Jack stood up and looked me in the eye. He looked so sorry, so despondent.

"I'm sorry, Rees. I had no idea. That bastards conned the both of us!"

He turned away and tripped over the beer crate! Quickly regaining his balance he left the shop. What a day this had been and it wasn't over yet.

A short while later Michael came into the shop. In the day light he looked even more forlorn. His clothes were rags, hanging off an emaciated body. He was filthy dirty! This would not do, something had to be done.

"Ello, Rees, I comes as you said to."

"Hello, Michael. You eaten today? Bit hungry myself now. What do you recommend?"

" 'Ave you eaten Jellied Eel, Rees? Good that is, I don't gets it much but I likes it when I do." Michael smiled. His bright eyes smiling out of a dirt laden face.

"I've eaten Cockles, Mussels and the Swansea speciality, Lava Bread, but I've never tried Jellied Eel. Where do we get some then?"

"Follow me, I knows a place." Michael answered.

It was all show on my part. I didn't want the lad to see how angry and upset I was. The beer had given me an appetite though. Locking up the shop I followed Michael. He led me through the narrow, dirty and foul smelling streets. The tall buildings blocking out much of the light so that we walked in shadows. Drunken people were every where. Some standing, others sleeping on the shit covered pavements. The unfortunate women plying their trade on every street corner. One even accosted me. She didn't look that old but she was clearly under the influence of alcohol.

" Fancy a good time mishter? I used to be an acrobat!" she giggled as she said it and then nearly lost her balance. Grabbing her arm I managed to stop her falling.

Fishing about in my pocket I found a sixpenny bit and gave it to her. She lifted her skirts and leaned against the wall with her arse to the wind! Hell, it was daylight and Michael was with me!

"NO! It's alright, take the money I don't need that."

She dropped her skirts, drunkenly smiled and meandered off down the street. What a place this is! Morriston really was better. Yes, it had its unfortunates but not on this scale.

"Alright there, Michael?" I asked, my voice betraying my shame.

"Yes, lets go get some Eels!"

My God, he wasn't shaken one bit! After walking a few more streets Michael stopped.

" 'Ere it is, the Eel shop."

I looked at the shop sign. Kelly's Pie And Eel shop! Surely this was just a coincidence, it had to be.

"Why this shop, Michael? It can't be the only one that sells Jellied Eels?" I questioned.

"Nah, it isn't but it sells the best ones. I'm starving, can we 'ave some Eels now?"

"Yes, come on then." I answered.

"Oi you, out of my shop!" A voice cried out.

Michael made to leave, I stopped him. He was a paying customer after all.

"He's with me. You have a problem with that? If so we'll go elsewhere." I said rather forcibly.

"Er...no...sorry. I didn't realise he was with you. What will it be?"

"What are we having, Michael? You can order."

The look on the her face was a picture. She was, I don't know, maybe thirty or even forty. Not pretty by any stretch of the imagination. Dark, greasy hair that hung from her head like a mass of rats tails. She had a fat face that seemed to squash her eyes into slits, a large nose covered in spots and fat, blubbery lips. I am not an unkind man but when she judged Michael on his appearance, well, got my goat that did. My ugly mood didn't help either.

"We'll 'ave two bowls of Jellies and some bread." Michael ordered.

We sat at a table by the window. Not that there was anything to see. There was nothing of interest going on in the dreary street outside. The bowls of Jellies arrived, brought to us my Miss Judgemental.

"That will be five pence." She said, sneering at Michael. With an air of dignity that he had probably never known before, Michael delved into his ragged trousers and produced a tanner.

"You can keep the change." He said to her with a smile as wide as a rainbow on his face.

The look on her face was a picture! Humiliated, she stormed off.

"Feel good, Michael?" I asked.

"Yep, Rees, I's never been able to do that before."

We both laughed and tucked into our Eels and bread. When we got back to the shop Jack's men were waiting.

"Sorry we're late boys, went for some grub."

I opened the door and we all trooped in. Giving instructions to the six men who quickly busied themselves around the shop, I gave Michael a quick tour of the building.

"It's huge! All these rooms. We only gots one room to live in."

"Who's we?" I asked him.

"My mother and me. I aint got a dad. Got killed down the docks before I was born he did."

"My dad got killed too. He worked in a big factory down in Swansea."

Michael gave me an understanding look. We had something in common at least.

"Where do you live, Michael?"

"Our room is in Miller's Court, number 13. One of McCarthy's rents it is. That's how I knows him. It's only a small place but keeps the rain out."

As he spoke I wondered how they managed to pay the rent. He was dressed in rags, was often hungry and dirty. Was his mother the same? I guessed that his mother was one of the many prostitutes that proliferated the area.

"I got to go now. My mother be wondering where I am."

I left the shop with him and as we were passing the bakers shop I quickly stepped inside. Michael stopped and looked at me through the window. A puzzled look on his face. I came out with a loaf of bread, a pat of butter and a few little cakes all carried in a large brown paper bag. A scratch cab coming down the street made a lot of noise. Stepping into the road I put my hand out. The cab stopped. Handing the bag to Michael I spoke to the driver.

"Here's five pence. Make sure the boy gets home safely."

"Right you are guv'nor".

"Thanks, Rees. My mother will think its her birthday when she sees this!" The tears welled in his eyes but didn't fall.

"I'll see you tomorrow, Michael."

He nodded to me as the cab pulled away.

The shop was a hive of activity when I returned. The shelves were being filled with various items, bars of soap, candles, bottles of bleach, bees wax polish etc. Wouldn't be much call for most of that around here. Eventually the job was finished. I paid the men three pennies each, more than the going rate but they had all worked hard. Looking at the shelves it was very apparent that I'd need to stock more of the basics and less of the luxuries such as soap! Jack came in a little while later, the smell of beer seeping out of his pores.

"Looks a little bare, Rees. Most of the shelves are empty. You need to get to the wholesalers down Dockside. Get all you need down there."

"Well, there's the problem. In Morriston I knew what to stock. Here, I haven't got a clue?"

"Any of that beer left? I'm fair parched."

"The crates over there look, in the corner." I told him.

With bottle in hand he leaned on the counter.

"Used to be a pub this place. The Blue Coat Boy. Damned silly name to call a boozer! Landlord got too fond of what he sold. Messed the business up he did. The bank took the building, he got thrown out. On the market for a few years it was. I got it cheap."

That explained the large 'shop' area. The long counter. The supporting pillars. The large windows. It all made sense now.

"I don't know what to do with it. As a shop it's too big. Wasting space that is." I said.

"It has potential, Rees, I'm sure you'll come up with something. I've been thinking too. In light of what's happened the rent will only be a shilling a week for now that is. If you make a fair profit then it'll go up. Now that's cheap for a building this size and you don't start paying until the shop is earning. I can't be any fairer than that. Keep it under your hat though, don't want people thinking that old Jack's gone soft in the head!"

The look on his face told me he was being serious. He took a swig of beer and thought for a moment. Gazing out of the large side window as he did so.

"I'm sending my man down to the wholesalers later. He can pick up some goods for you at the same time. I'll tell him to get double of what he normally gets for me. We can square up later."

"That would be helpful, thanks, Jack. Ask him to get me a tin bath and a couple of large buckets would you?"

Jack looked at me, shrugged his large shoulders, finished his beer and turned to leave.

"Expect a delivery later then." He said as he walked into the door frame!

"Fuck!" He exclaimed and walked off up the street.

An hour or so later a large wagon pulled up outside the shop. The driver dismounted, secured his horse and came into the shop.

"You, Rees?" He asked.

"Yes, I am. Is that for me?" I asked pointing to the wagon.

"Not the wagon or the 'orse but what's in it is!" He said, smiling.

I laughed and went to the window to see what was on the wagon. The tin bath stood upright in the back like a charioteer. Couldn't make out much else.

"I'm Harry, known as Indian Harry round these parts."

I shook the offered hand. "Rees, Rees Llewellyn. Pleased to meet you."

"Right, best get it unloaded." He said.

"I'll give you a hand, Harry."

Slowly the wagon was unloaded. Mysterious plywood boxes and packages soon piled up in the shop. By the time we finished the sweat was running down both our faces.

"Fancy a beer, Harry"

"Not half! Dry as dust my mouth is!"

Getting two bottles from the crate in the corner I handed one to Harry. Tops were popped and we both took hefty swigs. It wasn't long before the bottles were empty.

"Let's get this lot sorted then, Rees. See those plywood boxes, they are full of loose tea. People round here like to buy what they can afford. A penneth worth of tea is better than no tea."

I couldn't argue with that. Together we moved the box behind the counter and up against the wall beneath the shelves. Next came some of the packages which were placed on the counter top. Harry opened them up. Cutlery, knives, forks and spoons! The look on my face must have been a puzzled one.

"People do eat round here. Not everyone is a pauper. These are cheap ones, made of tin. Sell them as a set or separate. Ha'penny a piece or a penny a set."

The next package contained cheap tin plates and mugs. Was the tin made in Morriston I wondered?

"Sell them for sixpence a plate. You'll be surprised how many of those you sell. The large doss houses round here will be your best customers. The mugs, sell for them for a fourpence."

Harry retrieved a double ended hook and a small weighing scales out of the other plywood box. From one of the packages he took out a handful of cone shaped flat paper bags. He put the weighing scales on the counter in line with the box of tea. Taking the hook he hung one end from the shelf above the tea box he pushed the hook at the other end through the top edge of the pile of paper bags. Suspending them over the tea box.

"When a customer comes in for some tea. Weigh it out, a penny an ounce, rip the top bag off, shake it open, put the tea in the bag, screw the top shut and give it to the customer."

It didn't take long to get sorted. The shelves were not all full by any means but looked a lot better. Fire wood filled the lower shelves. Fires burn all year round, they are needed for cooking. Boxes of the tin cutlery, jars of various types of sweets, cigarettes and tobacco filled other shelves. Numerous boxes of candles stacked high on the top shelves. Harry told me that I would sell hundreds of candles a week because, like Morriston, many of the houses here did not have gas lamps. Wicker baskets tied to hooks hung in lines from top shelf to bottom.

"Harry, where can I get some coal?" I asked.

"There's a couple of bags on the wagon for Jack. He didn't say you wanted coal. I'll get one off for you, Jack won't mind."

"Thanks, Harry. I'll take the tin bath and the bucket through to the kitchen."

When I returned, a bag of coal stood in the middle of the floor. Harry had gone. Grabbing the sack around it's middle I staggered my way to the kitchen. Dai The Coal made it look so easy! Out in the yard I found the tap and filled the bucket with water. The stove was lit and burning nicely. I placed the bucket on the grid and went to get myself a beer. Sitting behind the counter I sipped my beer while the water heated up. I needed a bath badly. The water soon boiled and I poured into the small tin bath, a little cold water and it would be just right.

I scrubbed myself from top to bottom and with freshly boiled but now cooled water, rinsed myself off. Dressed in fresh, clean clothes I went to get some food. I soon found a cafe that looked fairly tidy. Inside it was filled with tables and chairs and was very busy. The menu sported the usual jellied Eels. Pie and mash was my choice. It was good, very good. I hadn't realised how hungry I was! Looking around at the people and the amount of money going into the till, gave mean idea. A shop come cafe. Why not? I paid the girl behind the counter for my meal and returned to my shop. The door squeaked as it opened. Need to oil the hinges.

Yes, it could work. There was more than enough room for a few tables and chairs. The stove was more than big enough to cook on and bake with. The thought of it was quite exciting. Darkness was starting to fall. I closed up the shop and went upstairs. Bed was calling me. It had been another busy day.

Michael came into the shop the following morning. He was not alone. A painfully thin woman was holding his hand. Her hair tied up around her head. Thin faced but she was very pretty. Small neat nose, and full sensuous lips. And those eyes, where had I seen those eyes before?

"Rees, this is my mother!" Michael exclaimed proudly. I noticed that his face was clean and that his clothes, although shabby, were not rags.

"Michael! Let me talk first. Where are your manners?"

The young lad looked at the floor, head bowed in admonishment.

"I want to thank you for your kindness, Mr Llewellyn. The bread and cakes were most welcome. But you must understand that I pay my own way. Money is a bit short right now but I will repay you."

"No, there's no need. Michael has been very helpful. Look at it as his wages."

She looked at me with a stunned look on her face. Her eyes filling with tears.

"Are you alright, Mrs........" I asked.

"Yes.....your accent.....it …. reminds me of someone. Doesn't matter it was a long time ago." She managed to say.

"I'm sorry I didn't mean to upset you, Mrs......." I tried again.

"Mrs Barnett, Mary Jane Barnett."

"Rees Llewellyn, at your service." I smiled my best smile.

Mary smiled back. She really was a lovely looking woman.

"I lost my husband years ago. Bad time that was especially as I was expecting Michael."

"Sorry to hear that, Mrs Barnett. Michael did tell me about his dad."

Mary reached out her hand and ruffled the boys hair.

"He's not a bad lad, looks after his mother as best he can. Hard for him it is though."

"Yes, I imagine it would be. I've a job for Michael, if its alright with you, Mrs Barnett?"

"Please, call me Mary. Mrs Barnett sounds so formal."

" Alright, Mary, it is. You can call me Rees. Now these windows need cleaning badly. I think Michael is up to the job. What do you say, Mary?"

" That's fine with me. I'll give him a hand, if that's alright with you? I haven't anything on at the moment."

Armed with a bucket of soapy water, a cloth each and a step ladder, mother and son set to work. It was hard work to get the windows clean. Mary cleaned the bottom halves while Michael cleaned the top halves, standing proudly on the step ladder.
I busied myself inside, sweeping the floor, polishing the counter and filling the buckets with clean water numerous times. When they had finished the windows sparkled.

"You've done a good job there. You could eat your dinner of those windows!" I said.

"Thank you, Rees. I'm really tired now. Hard work that was." Mary gave me a little smile.

"I'm starvin'." Michael said, rubbing his tummy.

Searching around my nearly empty trouser pockets, my hand closed on a few coins. Counting them I had the grand total of ten pence ha'penny. I handed the coins to Mary.

"Thank you for all your hard work."

"No, Rees, that's too much. I normally only get sixpence for cleaning work."

"Well, there's five pence for you and five pence for Michael with a little bonus thrown in for a job well done."

"Thank you, Rees, most kind of you. Now, how much do I owe you for the bread and the cakes?"

I gave a little laugh, she was a stubborn one.

"Nothing, part of the wages they are."

Mary opened her mouth as if to speak and then closed it.

"C'mon, let's go get some grub, I'm starvin'" Michael was eager to go, pulling at his mothers skirt."

Looking pleased but tired Mary took her sons hand and made to leave. Turning back to me as she did so.

"Good bye, Rees and thank you again."

She really was a good looking woman, needs a bit of fattening up but that's the only fault I could find. And those eyes, I just couldn't place where I'd seen them before. The memory was out of reach in my mind.

"Mary" I called out as they stepped out of the door.

"I'll be needing someone to help around here. Would you be interested?"

"Yes, Rees, I would. Money is short and we have to live. I don't..er....you know....walk the streets. So any chance to earn some money is welcome."

"Great! Can you start tomorrow?" I asked.

"There's a lot to be sorted, Mary. I haven't started on the upstairs yet."

"I'll see you tomorrow then." She said with a smile.

"Me too!" Exclaimed Michael excitedly.

I would have to open the shop soon so that people know that I'm here. Word of mouth and all that. But it had to be all sorted first. Even with the stock removed from the downstairs room it was still cluttered with packing cases, furniture and all things associated with a household. These would need to be taken upstairs and placed in the appropriate rooms. I can move the smaller items but I'll ask Jack if I can borrow a couple of his men to move the larger ones. My grandfather's table for a start. I wanted that in the kitchen, under the window, just as it was in Morriston.

It took me a while to move the smaller items upstairs. The room I chose as the living room now had a small table and four chairs. A thick brown oval rug on the floor. The table and chairs sat on top of it. A small side cabinet, a larger cupboard and the usual nic nacs of ornaments and the like. The two armchairs placed either side of the fire place. I nearly ruptured myself getting those up the stairs! My cot and the other smaller bedroom furniture I put in the room at the back of the building. I hoped that it would be a little quieter as it didn't face the street. The rest would have to wait until I had some help to move it. Locking up the shop and turning off the gas lamps I picked up the candle and went upstairs. I didn't bother lighting the lamps, a candle was sufficient. In my bedroom I quickly undressed, put on my night shirt and climbed into my cot. Sleep came fast, I was exhausted.

The following morning dawned damp and dreary. Making myself a cup of tea I sat on the stool behind the counter. The steam rising off the hot brew irritated my nose as I sipped it. A knock on the door startled me, my tea nearly ended up in my lap! Looking through the window I saw two men looking back at me. They were McCarthy's men. I recognised them as the widow board removers.

"Mornin'" I said cheerfully.

" Mornin' guv'nor. Jack says you got work for us."

"Aye, come on in and I'll show what needs to be done."

It didn't take them long to start shifting the larger furniture upstairs. It was amusing to see them wobbling under the weight of the large wardrobe as they slowly climbed the stairs. The job was soon done. I had a quick look around. Everything was where it was supposed to be. It actually looked like a home now.

In the shop I paid the men from my replenished pocket.

"Thanks guv'nor, much appreciated" said one.

"Yeah, thanks! My missus will be well pleased." said the other.

I'd given them sixpence each, not to be sniffed at but not a fortune either. Life here was hard for some.

Mary came into the shop shortly after the men had left. She looked radiant. Her long red tinged hair was hanging around her waist. It gently swayed as she moved. It shone even in the dull morning light. Her coat was presentable although it had seen better days. She was wearing mens boots!

"Good Morning, Rees. I see you've noticed the boots. Well, you wear what you can get around here. With all the shit and muck, boots are the best."

"Morning, Mary. Sorry, I didn't mean any offence. Took me by surprise that's all."

Her face softened and she smiled a little. She looked at me a few seconds, a questioning look.

"Are you from Cardiff, Rees? Your accent reminds me of my mothers."

"No, Swansea. Didn't Michael tell you?"

"He doesn't tell me a lot, Rees. Living here it's best I suppose. I don't want to know what he sees and hears."

Having experienced it myself I understood what she meant.

"Anyway. Rees, I'm here to work not gossip. Where do you want me to start?" Mary asked.

"In the back rooms please, Mary."

I led her behind the counter and through to the first room to be cleaned. It was a mess. Empty packing crates, paper, old sheets I'd used to wrap things up in lay all over the floor.

"It's a mess, but if you put the paper and old sheets into the packing cases and have a sweep up that would be a help."

" I can do that, Rees. Off you go then, let a woman get on with her job."

With a smile I left her to it and returned to the shop where my first customer was waiting!

"Morning, how can I help you?" I politely asked.

He pointed at the shelf where the tobacco and cigarettes were displayed. Perhaps he was a mute and couldn't speak? I shrugged my shoulders to indicate that I didn't understand. He gave a loud sigh and pulled a clay pipe from his jacket pocket. Holding it in front of me and pointing at it he said in a very thick accent.

"Pipe smoke."

Pipe smoke? Ah, pipe tobacco! But which one did he want? I pointed to the various pouches of tobacco until he said.

"Ja, das ist gut" (Yes, that is good.)

Pointing again to make certain and getting a nod of approval I handed him the tobacco pouch.

"That will be a fourpence ha'penny, please."

He put his hand in his trouser pocket, pulled it out and offered me a palm filled with various coins. There was a shilling there! The man had no idea of the value of coins he held!

At that moment a young girl ran into the shop.

"Opa, was machst du?" She asked the old man.

 (Grandfather, what are you doing?)

"Ich kaufe Pfeifentabak."

(I'm buying pipe tobacco.)

The girl looked at me apologetically.

"Sorry mister. He's my grandfather, never goes out on his own normally. He hasn't been here long and as you see he doesn't speak English. How much does he owe you?"

"Fourpence ha'penny but I could have robbed him of his shilling had I a mind to."

"Thank you. Not many honest people round here."

Taking the old man by the arm she led him out of the shop.

Living here is going to take some getting used to! I could hear Mary at work in the back room. The sound of paper being scrunched up, either in her hands or being pushed into the packing cases. The noises made by a busy woman. I wanted to go and watch her work but I resisted the temptation. I did find her interesting, no doubt about that, but I doubt that she felt the same about me.

"Mary, where's Michael this morning?" I asked entering the room where she was busy sweeping the smaller bits of paper and a considerable amount of dirt into a small heap.

"Doing a few errands for Jack. He'll be here when he's done with that. It's worth a penny or two to him, Rees."

"Fair enough, just wondering. I'll leave you to it then."

"Wait, Rees. Can you hold the dustpan while I brush this mess onto it?"

Taking hold of the dust pan I knelt down and placed it in front of the small heap, which Mary promptly swept on to it. I looked up at her as she did. Her grey eyes glistened, irritated by the dust.

Where the hell had I seen those eyes before?

I heard a call from the shop, an impatient voice "Ello, any body here?"

"Better go see to your customer, Rees." Mary said smiling.

"Sorry, how can I help you?" I said entering the shop.

" Ello deary, I need a bit o' thread. Stockings got another bloody hole in them again!" She exclaimed.

"Bit of thread, sorry I don't........" Mary came in to the shop.

" 'Ello Polly, love. How are you, darlin'? A pennies worth is it?" she asked.

"Yes, that'll do me, sweet heart, just need to sew up the hole. It's these boots see, too big and rubs me toes they do."

Mary walked a little way down the the length of the counter until she came to the shelf were the box of cotton reels were kept. Picking up a reel of black cotton she deftly wound a few coils around her finger. Pushing me gently aside she pulled off one of paper cone bags that were meant for the tea, and gently removing the coil of cotton from her finger, placed in the bag and handed it to Polly.

"There you are, Polly, that'll be a penny, love. Oh, and you might want to pack some newspaper into those boots, stops them rubbing." Mary sounded very professional as she spoke. How did she know this poor woman I thought?

"Thank you my lovely, it's a hard life, Mary, but we survives how we can." She handed over the penny and went on her way.

"Mary, how did you know that? The length of cotton, the poor woman's name, how? And she knew your name." The confusion must have been very evident on my face.

"Polly is an old friend of my mothers, Rees. She used to look after me sometimes when I was a baby."

I wanted to ask more but decided against it. None of my business anyway.

"You have a lot to learn , Rees. People around here only buy what they can afford, if they manage the doss houses, they may buy more but they still only buy what they need. It's the way of life in these parts. I've helped out in Jacks shop many a time, I know how it works." She gave me a knowing look, a look that got my heart beating a little faster. I think I am falling for Mary Jane Barnett.

Two weeks later.

Trade had picked up considerably but it needed to be far more. My Morriston shop took three times as much money as this one. Once the rent and wages were paid I was just about breaking even. Mary worked in the shop now on top of her cleaning duties. She knew these people and could understand their needs far better than me. Michael helped when he could after school, I paid for his schooling. Mary was very reluctant at first but my perseverance paid off. She understood that education was his only chance out of this hell hole. Memories of little Timmy played on my mind. He would probably end up a minion in that man consuming machine of Copperopolis. I was determined that Michael would have a better chance in life.

Jack came into the shop and handed me an envelope. It was from my solicitor in Morriston, the address printed on the back of the envelope. Although my address was on the front of the envelope the post was delivered to Jack as he was my landlord.

The posties new this apparently? This would be the confirmation of the Morriston shop sale. And not before time. I wasn't short of money yet thanks to my grandfather, he'd left me a tidy sum but it was dwindling at an alarming rate.

I opened the envelope and read the letter it contained.

Dear Mr Llewellyn,

We are pleased to inform you that as per your instructions, via your London solicitors, Messrs Churchill, Anderson & Warren, the necessary confirmation having been obtained, the sum of seventy seven pounds from the sale of the Morriston premises has been paid to Mr John Kelly.

We trust that this is in order and thank you for your custom.

With regards...........

I fell back onto the stool and nearly toppled off it!

"What's up, Rees! You look like you've seen a ghost." Jack said as he leaned over the counter to grab me should I fall. He took the letter out of my trembling hand. As he read it I saw his anger build. He started to tremble, his face turned purple, I felt sure he would suffer a fit or something. Turning away from me he threw his arms up.

"Rees, as god is my witness, I will kill that fuckin' runt, of that you have my word. I told you, Rees, I fuckin' told you! He's in the shit again, it's taken a long time but he's definitely in it up to his fuckin' neck no doubt."

I said nothing, too stunned and too disappointed by the man I once considered a friend. Jack left, still ranting I wouldn't want to be his opponent in the bare knuckle fight he was due to participate in later.

What the hell do I do now?

There was no point in taking legal action, I would be throwing good money after bad. John wouldn't be in Morriston, not after this. He could be any where by now. Mary came out of the passage way, looked at me and went back to her cleaning duties. If my face reflected may rage then I don't blame her.

The next morning I left Mary in charge of the shop and went to see Jack. I had made some decisions that needed his approval. Walking through the filthy streets filled with ragged, dirty houses, which were in turn filled with their ragged, dirty occupants wasn't a pleasant experience. I don't think I'll ever get used to it or the smell either. Dorset Street, you'd think a street named after a pleasant part of the English countryside would be equally as pleasant. It wasn't, it was one of the worst streets in the area. Even at this early hour the addicted folk were sat amongst the filth of the pavement. The unfortunates patrolling. Pushing the door I entered Jack's shop. He was reading a newspaper that was spread out on the counter. He looked up as I walked in.

"Rees, do I wish you a good morning or not?"

"Mornin', Jack. I've been doing some thinking, there's no point in me pursuing, John, it would just cost me more money for nothing. He won't be in Morriston now, he could be anywhere."

"Makes sense, Rees, Kelly isn't stupid, he wouldn't stay in a place where he would be easily found. Probably be in France by now. The fuckin' little runt!"

"Probably, so I've decided to branch out. Turn the shop into a shop come cafe. It will specialise in Welsh food, namely Swansea pies and Cawl, Welsh soup that is, Jack."

"Sounds like a plan, Rees, where do I come into it?"

" I'm going to need the shop front repaired, the rotten woodwork replaced and then painted dark green. I'll need a sign writer to do the shop/cafe name in bold letters in red. I'm going to call it; The Welshman. What do you think?"

"I like it, Rees. I'll get on to my people right away. I'm not paying for it though, not wishing to be unsympathetic but that sort of alteration is going to cost and I don't want to spend money on a business that may not succeed. You can understand that can't you?"

"Yes, of course, I didn't expect you to pay, Jack, just wanted the go ahead that's all. I'll leave it to you to arrange then. The sooner the better I need the challenge to take my mind off things."

Two months later.

The shop/cafe looked wonderful. The dark green painted wood work gave it a homely feel and above the front windows, in bold red lettering the name: The Welshman. People came from all over the area to have a look. Many said that it was the smartest looking shop around. I think Jack was a little peeved but he didn't show it.

He said that the transformation was astounding; that he could never have imagined it to look so good. Inside it had been painted out as-well. The iron columns painted the same dark green and the grape design at their tops painted red. Twelve tables and forty eight chairs now filled the area to the left of the shop. The smell of Swansea pies and cawl filled the air. And it was very busy.

The locals and those from further afield kept Mary very busy, not only with the cooking but the taking of orders and waiting on the tables. I need more staff so that Mary can concentrate on the cooking. I helped out as much as I could but that wasn't enough. The pies were the main seller.

Keeping up with demand was a nightmare! Grandfather's recipe was a winner with the customers. And at threepence a pie was cheap as well. The meat was bought from Smithfield Market which was not that far away so transportation costs were low. The vegetables for the cawl and the pies were bought from the nearby Spitalfields market. As my costs were low I could sell at a cheaper price. A large bowl of cawl was only fourpence ha'penny.

Cawl is a Welsh speciality, a soup made of Lamb neck fillets cut into chunks, swede, carrots, potatoes, parsnip and leek. All boiled up in a huge cast iron cauldron that Jack got for me. It only just fitted on the cooker and Mary was constantly preparing the ingredients for the next batch as the cauldron didn't take long to empty. It was the same with the pies, a constant process of making pastry, cutting it to fit the pies moulds, ladling out the filling from another large pot, adding the lids and placing them in the large oven. In went the trays out came the baked pies. Poor Mary was worked off her feet. Washing the dishes that soon piled up in the large sink was another problem. Something would have to be done.

The Welshman always closed at five thirty in the afternoon. Although there was more than enough custom to stay open much later, we were too exhausted to do it.

"Rees, we need extra staff. We can't cope with the demand on our own. Even with Michael helping wash the dishes after school its near impossible to keep up. I'm worn out!"

And she looked it, poor thing. Flour speckled her hair and face. vegetable juices and meat juices stained her morning clean apron. She looked at me weariness etched on her face, but she managed a smile. She'd put on some weight and was a very comely woman. I don't know if she noticed me looking but she suddenly looked away.

"How about a nice cup of tea, carriad?" I innocently asked.

Her head snapped around and she looked at me sternly, her steel grey eyes glaring at me.

"Don't ever call me that again, Rees, never!" and she stormed off out of the cafe and melted into the crowd.

What did I do? I had no idea. Closing up the cafe I went back into the kitchen and finished up washing the dishes and cleaning out the pot and cauldron.

A week later.

The girls that were recommended by; The Sisters Of Mercy, soon got the hang of things. Mary had suggested that I contact the Sisters as they helped destitute girls find employment.

I'd changed the way we worked. The tables weren't waited on now. The customer gave his or her order at the counter and took the pies or soup back to the table. That saved a lot of time.

Mary now had a girl to help with the cooking and one girl stayed at the counter. Things were going much more smoothly, the stress had gone, it was all working well, like the well oiled cogs of a machine. Mary was still treating me rather coolly. A good morning was about all the conversation I had with her. It couldn't go on like that. I closed up the cafe and waited for Mary to finish up the cleaning. The new staff had already left. Mary came out. Coat on and ready to leave.

"May I have a word please, Mary?" I asked in a gentle voice.

She stopped, head down and looking at the floor.

"I don't know what I did to upset you but what ever it was, I'm sorry. I thought we were friends?"

She looked up, those eyes glistening. She took me by the arm and led me to a table. She motioned me to sit down and she sat opposite.

"My mother used to call me carriad, Rees. That's why I got so upset. We came to this shit hole from Cardiff. She got herself pregnant with me and her family threw her out. I was only a toddler, they waited until I was a year or two old, probably to ease their religious souls rather than out of kindness."

She told me the whole story of how her mother struggled to keep a roof over their heads. How she had to walk the streets to put food on the table and how she was often left with her mothers friends while she plied her trade down in Docklands or Limehouse.

"Hard for me it was, Rees. My mother always said that she had no choice. If I don't do it we starve, carriad. And when you called me carriad it brought it all flooding back. That's why I was so upset."

"Where is your mother now, Mary?" It was an obvious question to ask.

"She died when I was eight years old. The Sisters Of Mercy took me in. I stayed with them until I was sixteen."

She gazed out of the window, lost in thought. Then she continued.

"I left and found work as a maid with a rich Jewish family. Nice family they were, treated me well. It was there that I met Joseph, my husband to be. And to cut a long story short we got married, I fell pregnant with Michael and then Joseph got killed in an accident down the docks."

She reached over and took my hand in hers. I was very surprised at that but didn't say anything.

"It was hard, Rees, I worked when I could at what ever was available but I never walked the streets. We may have been poor but I paid the rent and fed us as much as was possible. Yes, there were times when we didn't eat for a day or two but for me it was better to go hungry than sell myself. It may have come to it, I'm sure it would have, but then you came along and saved the both of us." She looked at me with such gratitude that I knew I was blushing.

"No, Mary. You saved yourself and Michael. I just helped out a little. Now no more talk of that nature. I hear that Jack has new lodgings for you?"

"Yes, up in Berner Street, one of the better streets around here. Two ground floor rooms in a nice house. Rent is a lot more but I can afford it now, thanks to you."

She let go of my hand and stood up, moving around the table she leaned over and kissed me on the forehead.

"Bless you, Rees Llewellyn." And walking quickly off, she left.

Autumn 1888.

The Welshman was now well known, not only in Spitalfields and Whitechapel but in the City and beyond. Many of the City people referred to it as; The Welshman In Whitechapel. Business was brisk, Mary and the rest of the staff working non stop to keep up with the demand.

People queued outside of the cafe and down the street. I paid a man to clean the pavement twice a day, can't have my customers standing in horse shit and what not. My time was taken up with the shop side of the enterprise, the cafe customers often buying from the shop, tobacco and cigarettes mainly but candles and tea sold well too.

My bank account had grown into a very respectable sum. I could be considered to be a rather wealthy man. Who would have thought that a little over three years ago when I first saw the shop that it would turn out like this. I could retire if I wished and lead an easy life but that wasn't for me. I enjoyed working in the shop too much and the fact that I saw Mary every day was a bonus. Regular meals, over the years, mainly of pie and cawl had put the flesh back on her bones.

And with the money she earned the luxuries previously beyond her means had made a difference to her complexion. She reminded me of Mrs Jenkins, little Timmy's mother in many ways except for the eyes.

"Rees." Mary called out. "We need more coal and lamb fillets when you have a minute."

The coal was kept in the cellar, it was poured in through the coal hole in the pavement. A round hole covered with a cast iron grating. The lamb was kept in the cold store. I got the lamb first and took it into the kitchen where two of the kitchen girls, Victoria and Emily, took it off me and put it on the meat table ready for cutting. The cellar was accessed through a trap door set into the floor behind the counter. Carrying the large coal scuttle made descending the rickety steps down to the cellar very difficult and getting back up with the full scuttle even worse! Just as I came back into the shop after my role play as 'Dai The Coal' Jack entered.

"Hello, Rees. Busy again I see. Thanks to you most of the shops around here are busier. Bringing in the custom you are." He smiled. "I've come for the rent, Harry can't make it"

Reaching in to the till for a handful of coins I counted out five shillings and gave the coins to Jack, who promptly produced a rent book, filled in the payment details and signed it in front of me.

"All in order, Jack. Now, do you think I could have a bowl of that delicious soup?"

"Of course, Jack, go through to the kitchen, Mary or one of the girls will sort you out."

1ˢᵗ September 1888.

Mary came hurtling into the cafe like a train with no brakes.

"Rees, have you heard the news? Terrible it is, a woman's been found murdered down in Bucks Row."

 She couldn't hide the panic in her face." Bloody scary it is."

"Have a sit down, Mary. There's a pot of tea brewing. I'll lock the door for ten minutes, you need to calm yourself."

After the cup of tea Mary calmed a little. I opened up the cafe and the customers came in. The conversation was all about the murder, that it must be a mad man or an escaped animal or a Jew. The cafe was still very busy, people still venturing out and about. If anything it got a little busier than usual, if that were possible, as people came into the area to view the murder site and to listen to the gossip. A few of the unfortunate women were talking on the street corner just outside of the cafe.

It appears that the murdered woman was one of their sisters, a poor unfortunate just trying to survive. All around the vicinity people talked of the terrible murder. In the cafe they talked about the murder, in between mouthfuls of pie or cawl!

The murder was still the main topic of conversation a few days later. The people were shocked that such a terrible crime could be committed out in the open. Jack came into the shop looking very distressed.

"What's up, Jack? You don't look so good."

"They've released the name of the murdered woman, Rees. You knew her and so does Mary. I knew her too. Harmless old drunk she was, wouldn't hurt a fly. She was Polly Nichols."

I sat down on the stool. Not Polly! she came into the shop quite often over the years. Normally for thread, sometimes for a penneth worth of soap. But mostly for the free pot of soup I used to discreetly hand to her. She'd eat it outside, bring the pot back and with a wave and a "Ta ta, old cock." off she'd go.

"Thanks for bringing the news, Jack. I'd better tell Mary before the gossip mongers do."

Mary literally collapsed on hearing the news, great big sobs racked her body. I led her into the other room, now the store room and sat her down on a packing case.

"Oh, Rees, not Polly. I've known her for years. She was a friend of my mother. She used to look after me when my mother couldn't. Oh my god, poor Polly!"

She starting sobbing again. I put my arms around her and held her close. She buried her head into my chest and sobbed uncontrollably. I realised then that I loved her but it was not the time to say it and the time would probably never be right. I said nothing. I held her until the sobbing stopped. She pushed away from me and wiping her eyes looked at me. Those eyes were wet with tears as were her cheeks.

"I'm alright, Rees, let me up I have work to do." She pushed passed me and returned to the kitchen. Best thing perhaps, keep her mind occupied. I didn't know it then but things were about to get a lot worse.

The next few days were really busy. People were flocking into the area to see where the 'poor unfortunate' as many of the papers referred to Polly as, was murdered. Even the toffs all decked out in their best came down to see the murder site. Made me bloody mad, fuckin' ghouls!

8th September

Barely a week later there was another murder. This one far worse than that of Polly. The poor victim was ripped open! Her intestines pulled out! This was unbelievable, one murder was bad enough, but two in the same area and the second one such a gruesome affair. When the victims name was released word of it soon spread and when the name reached Mary's ears she was inconsolable.

"My god, Rees, she was Annie Chapman, another of my mothers friends. What the hell is going on? It's as if the killer is targeting her old friends, but why?"

"Hang on, Mary. Your mothers been dead for sixteen years or there about, why would the killer be targeting them? No, it's just a coincidence and nothing more. You're in shock, your mind is playing games with you. Go home, that would be the best place for you right now." I said as forcibly as I could.

"No, Rees. I need to be here among friends and I need to be occupied. I'll collect Michael from school if that's alright?"

"Yes, of course, no problem." I patted her shoulder, gave her what I hoped was a reassuring smile and went back into the shop.

Mary

I left the cafe to pick up Michael. The murders were really playing on my mind. I just couldn't shake the feeling that they were personal. It was irrational, as Rees said to me, my mother died a long time ago, they could not be related. As I approached the school I noticed a confrontation. An old man trying to pull a young boy away with him! I started to run and as I got closer I saw that the young boy was Michael! I screamed out his name. The man looked at me, released Michael, and ran off.

"Michael are you alright? Come here, let me hold you. Who the hell was that man?"

"I don't know, never seen him before in my life. He kept telling me that he was my grandfather and that I had to go with him!"

That was enough for me, grabbing my son firmly by the arm we ran back to the cafe. Bursting through the door I shouted out for Rees. The customers looked at me in surprise, I didn't care. My son had suffered an attempted abduction....I just wanted Rees!

Rees.

Mary barrelled through the door dragging Michael with her. She kept shouting my name. What the hell had happened? Seeing me come out from the back room, she ran straight towards me.

"Rees!" she cried out. "He nearly got Michael. He was waiting for him outside the school. If I had been a few minutes later he would have taken him!"

"Calm down, Mary and tell me what happened." I said in a soothing tone, placing my hands on her shoulders as I did so.

Guiding them both in to the store room and finally getting Mary to calm down, she told me what she saw and what Michael had told her. It was an incredulous tale, almost unbelievable, if it wasn't for the shocked state that both Mary and Michael were in I would have said that it was imagined. Turning to look at Michael, who was visibly shaken, I asked him.

"You didn't recognise the man, he wasn't a local?"

"Never seen him before in my life, scared the hell out of me he did."

"Can you describe him, Michael?" I pensively asked.

"He was about your height but very dirty and he smelled bad. I was too busy trying to escape, Rees, I didn't take much notice of anything else. I'm sorry. And when my mother shouted out he let go of me and ran off. He said he was my grandfather, I aint got a grandfather."

"We'd better inform the police, safe and not sorry and all that. The other girls can mind the cafe. Hopefully, we won't be too long."

Commercial Street police station was a large, three storey building that was rather impressive. We walked in through the main entrance and up to the front desk. There were a few other people sat in the waiting area but it was surprisingly empty.

"Can I help you?" The desk sergeant asked. Mary pushed forward and explained the whole situation, from the murdered women who were once friends of her mother, to the abduction attempt on Michael. The sergeant carefully writing it all down in the ledger on the desk. When Mary had finished telling the tale, the desk sergeant did as I had already done, questioned certain points for clarification.

"I've logged your statement but I wouldn't read too much into the situation." He said. " The murdered woman being friends of your mother can only be coincidence, the years having passed and all. As for the man who tried to take Michael, probably an old soak with the deliriums, thought that the boy was his grandson." He looked at Mary and must have seen something in her face.

"We're a bit pushed what with these murders and all but I'll get the school area patrolled at finishing time, just to be on the safe side. I doubt it happen again though."

"Thank you, sergeant. I'll be there as-well. I'm not taking any chances." Mary said.

Life returned to a form of normality for the next few days. Mary was kept busy in the cafe, I was kept occupied in the shop. The police patrolled the school at finishing time and there was no further abduction attempt on Michael.

The people crowding into Spitalfields was unbelievable. Hanbury Street, where poor Annie was found murdered, was blocked by a huge throng of people that must have numbered in their hundreds. The police were having a hell of a job controlling the mass of people in order that the carts could get through.

All people talked about was the murders. Obviously the unfortunate women were scared. As of yet the police had no clue as to who the killer was. The patrols had been increased, house to house enquiries were being made. It was not through a lack of effort that the police had found nothing, it seemed that there was nothing to find. The killer was like an invisible man, not seen and not heard. The newspapers were selling out of copy in minutes. The newspaper boys having to frequently return to the printers to pick up more. They were not the only ones to profit from the terrible murders, my trade had increased to the point where I was having to turn people away, the cafe staff just couldn't cope with it. The street vendors were doing a roaring trade. I'd noticed the hot potato seller frequently leaving his cart and returning with a bag of potatoes slung over each shoulder. Cheeky bugger had set up his cart opposite the cafe, can't blame him really, money is money at the end of the day.

30th September.

What the hell was that noise? Bang!....bang!....bang! "Rees! Wake up for christ's sake." Jack shouted as he hammered on the front door.

I got up, threw my clothes on, hopping on the landing trying to put my shoes on at the same time. Racing down the stairs, through the passageway and into the shop I could just make out Jack in the dim glow of the gas light opposite. I had no sooner opened the door when Jack grabbed me firmly by the shoulders.

" There's been two more murders, Rees. One in Berner Street the other in the city."

Berner Street.....Mary! I took off like a bat out of hell, Jack shouted something but I was too focused on getting to Mary to hear what it was. Jack ran after me and when we arrived in Berner Street it was full of people and police. Pushing through the crowds we arrived at Mary's lodgings. I knocked on the door shouting her name over and over again. I was about to kick the door in, much to Jack's dismay, when it opened. The sight that greeted me broke my heart. Mary stood in front of me, ashen faced and trembling, she was looking at me but not seeing me. Michael was held tight with an iron grip at her side.

"Mary...Mary, I said softly, It's me, Rees, and Jack is here. Can we come in?"

She seemed to come to her senses a little and led us in to the living room, holding Michael tightly all the while. Before either Jack or myself could speak Mary did.

"He's coming for me Rees, I know he is. He murdered that woman in a yard only four doors down. It's a message, I know it is...I'm next!"

She collapsed onto a chair by the small table that was pushed up against the wall opposite the fire place. I went to comfort her but she shook her head and continued to talk.

"He killed Polly and Annie, my mothers friends. He attempted to snatch Michel. He killed that woman tonight just doors away from me. He's coming for me, Rees, I know he is!" The look on her face was one of abject terror.

I didn't want to believe it, it couldn't be, but there was no getting around it, Mary's conclusion was a strong possibility.

"Mary, there's something else I have to tell you. Another woman was also killed tonight up in the city. Where, Jack?"

"Mitre square so the gossip says."

Mary sank further into the chair. Poor Michael who was sat in the other chair said nothing, his gaze fixed, his body unmoving. A bad case of shock no doubt.

"You can't stay here just in-case you're right and he is coming for you. Both of you must stay with me until the police catch the killer. Jack, can you find anyone to stay with us as-well, a chaperone?"

"Aye, old Mrs Maxwell lovely old dear she is, she'd be only too willing to help out, especially for the pies and soup." Jack's attempt to lighten the mood a little didn't work and it clearly embarrassed him.

"We'll need two beds, Jack, can you manage that? Michael can sleep on the cot. But I can't have Mary and Mrs Maxwell sleeping on the floor!"

"Not a problem, Rees. I've got some furniture in storage, I'll get on it as soon as we get back."

I expected Mary to refuse and cause a fuss, she didn't. Gathering some clothes together for herself and Michael and putting them in a small case. We were ready to go. Jack said he'd have one of his men to keep an eye on the lodging, just in case. We trooped out of Berner Street and made our way back to The Welshman.

We didn't notice the scruffy, dirty old man with his bloodied hands hidden in his pockets and the blood on his clothes concealed amongst the other filth and the darkness of the hour, watching us intently as we left. A hateful sneer on his face.

True to his word, Jack sent the extra beds and his men soon had them upstairs where Mrs Maxwell and Mary made them up. Jack's description of Mrs Maxwell was spot on, she was a lovely old dear. I'd have push the two armchairs together, front end to front to make a bed, a bit make shift but it would have to do. The privacy arrangements for bathing etc. could be sorted later. Hopefully, it won't be too long before this is over.

I was so glad that the cafe was busy, really busy, as it meant that Mary didn't have time to think. Michael was helping out too, it was decided to keep him home from school until the killer was caught. I was waiting for the names of the victims to be released, praying that they wouldn't be connected to Mary in any way. Jack came in often just to see that we were alright. I'd heard a lot of stories about Jack over the years. How he was this hardened criminal, a pimp, a bent landlord, illegal bare knuckle fighter, too many tales to tell. In the three years that I'd known him nothing could be further from the truth. Always helpful, especially in the recent week or so, yes, likes his beer and is a bit rough and ready, but if he was as the stories say he is then I never saw that side of him.

The newspapers were having a field day, the newspaper vendors crying out "Jack The Ripper, ladies and gentlemen, one penny. Read all about it!" Now all conversations were about this mysterious 'Jack The Ripper' The murders were now affecting some business's, especially those that stayed open late.

Come night fall many people went home, the streets virtually empty in some parts.

As The Welshman closed early business was not affected at all. The number of people coming into the area sight seeing had dwindled a little, fear of the killer was not confined just to Spitalfields and Whitechapel but throughout the principality. A petition had even been sent to Queen Victoria herself asking her to do something for the poor folk of the East End. The do-gooders and the charitable high lighting the conditions that some of them lived in and calling for social reform. Radical groups baying for the heads of those they thought responsible and generally stirring up trouble. It was the Jews who were in the firing line most of the time. As it was thought that no 'English' man could commit such crimes then the killer must be a Jew.

A piece of apron from the second victim of what was now being called 'The Double Event' was found in a doorway in Goulston Street. Inside the doorway some graffiti was written which read: The Jews are the men that will not be blamed for nothing. Anti Jewish feeling was running high. I hope they catch this bastard soon for everyone's sake, but especially for Mary.

Jack came in early one morning, a few days after the double murders. I could see by the look on his face that he had some news. There were a few early birds sat in the cafe having cawl for breakfast so he leaned over the counter and spoke quietly.

"The names of the last victims have been released. The one in Berner Street was Elizabeth Stride. The Mitre Square victim was Catherine Eddowes. Rees, I'm not a religious man, but I pray that those names are not known to Mary. I don't think her mind could take it."

"That makes two of us, Jack. Come on through and we'll soon find out." My stomach was in knots, a silent prayer said in my mind.

Jack went into the store room while I called Mary out of the kitchen. She was dappled with flour as she usually was and had bits of pastry stuck to her hands and fingers. She tried to rub if off on her apron but it was stuck like glue. She looked at me quizzically as I asked to go into the store room. Jack smiled as we entered.

"Hello, Mary, you alright?" he gently asked.

"Holding up, Jack. What's this all about?"

"The names of the victims have been released. We thought that you'd want to know, considering......"

"Just tell me, Jack. I have to know!" Mary exclaimed.

"The one in Berner Street, her name was Elizabeth Stride, do you know that name?"

Mary thought for a few moments staring into space as she did so. Eventually she said "No, I don't know that name. Tell me the other name."

"The second one was Catherine Eddowes."

As she heard the name her knees buckled. I rushed forward and caught her before she fell. Sitting her on a wooden box I waited for her to recover from the shock. She was visibly shaking.

"My god, Rees. Catherine Eddowes, or Cathy, was also a friend of my mothers. In better times, Polly, Annie, Cathy, mother and me used to go hopping in Kent. Every summer we used to go, stay for a few weeks. The fresh air did us good and we could earn a few shillings."

Jack turned and looked at me. I knew what he was thinking as I was thinking the same. Mary was the target! The killer was setting her up, frightening her, letting her know that he knew about her past and her mother and her friends. Without a word Jack left.

"Mary we need to talk to the police again, they need to know about this. We'll go as soon as Emily and Victoria arrive."

She stood up, placed her arms around me and squeezed hard, quite strong she was too. She kissed me quickly on the cheek.

"I can't thank you enough, Rees. I don't know what I'd do without you and Jack."

"Don't be silly, Mary. This has come as one hell of a shock to you, Michael and all of us. I can keep you safe here. Jack has got some of his men out on the streets patrolling. The police are out in huge numbers. This maniac will be caught, Mary, you can be sure of that."

She seemed to regain her composure, pulling herself upright, head up and shoulders back. A flour dappled soldier I thought to myself and chuckled despite it all. A tap on the door and Jack came in accompanied by two other men.

"Mary, I hope you don't mind but I went to the police station explained everything again including the recent developments. As soon as the desk sergeant heard the new developments he went into a back room and a few minutes later he returned with these two men. They are police officers and wish to speak to you."

Both men removed their hats as they looked at Mary. She did look a bit of a sight what the flour dappled all over her and the pastry stuck to her hands.

"Mary?" The older of the two asked. "I'm Inspector Abberline and this is Sergeant Thicke. We'd just like to ask you a few questions if that's alright?" Mary nodded her consent.

"Can you think of anyone that your mother may have known that may be holding a grudge, even after all these years? Think hard, Mary, this is important." Abberline asked firmly but kindly.

"I have thought about it, Inspector, and the only people I can think of are my mothers own family. They threw her out onto the streets once I was old enough to walk, the shame of it you see, unmarried mother, daughter of a respectable religious family, the gossip, the scorn of the neighbours and the community. My mother told me all this when I was old enough to understand."

"I see and how long ago was this, Mary?"

"Must be about twenty years or more, Inspector."

"And how did you both end up in Spitalfields?"

"My mother told me that London would be good for us, lots of work as it was such a big place. She scraped the money together and brought us here.

There were no real jobs for a young mother with a toddler. We ended up living in a hovel. She worked the streets to keep a roof over our heads. The streets eventually killed her and at the age of around eight I was taken in by the nuns."

"Is this line of questioning really necessary, Inspector?" I innocently asked.

Abberline turned to look at me "Yes, it is. I'm looking for anything that Mary may remember that could be a clue. The killer may or may not be targeting Mary but he seems to be targeting her mothers friends and I would really like to know why."

More questions and answers followed until Mary had told Abberline everything, including her marriage, her husbands death, all of her life laid bare.

"If you think of anything else that you consider may be of relevance come down to the station and ask for me."

Inspector Abberline and Sergeant Thicke wished us a good day and I showed them out. I returned to the storeroom, Jack and Mary were discussing the interview.

"Well, that was a waste of bleedin' time, hasn't sorted nothing has it? Jack said, his face a picture of disappointment.

"No, but it has got me thinking. Some of what my mother told me, well, it doesn't make sense. I mean why come here? She could have stayed in Cardiff, god knows it's big enough to get lost in. And then there's her accent, I thought nothing about it until I met Rees. He has the same accent that my mother had and Rees is Swansea born. I hadn't paid much attention to that but all the questioning, it's making me wonder."

"I wouldn't read too much into that, Mary. I've met many people from outside of Swansea who's accents would make them people of the town." I said .

"Yes, I know, Rees. This whole business has got me wound up tighter than a drum. Shall we get back to work, I need to be busy."

Mary returned to the kitchen where Emily and Victoria were hard at work.

"What the hell do you make of all this, Rees, because it's got me fair bollocksed to be honest?" Jack asked.

"I don't know what to think, Jack, I really don't. But one things for certain, I will not be letting Mary or Michael out of my sight!"

"Got a soft spot for her haven't you? Come on, Rees, anyone who looks close enough will see it a mile off."

"I can't deny it, Jack, I'm in love with her, but that is strictly between us, it goes no further....understand!"

He smiled, gave me a wink and made his way out, turning as he stepped through the door he said

 "I've got some of my men on patrol around here. Anyone who doesn't fit in they'll soon spot them. The coppers do their best but half of the buggers have been drafted in from outside of the area, they haven't got a bloody clue!"

October 1888.

As the days of October came and went with no further murders the people settled down a little. The unfortunates back on the streets in almost the same numbers as before the murders. People milling through the streets going about the business of every day life. The hot potato seller surrounded by customers clamouring for his attention. I watched him frantically serving one after another, hot potatoes out of the oven and fresh potatoes put in.

One dishevelled old man sat on the step of a run down building, slowly eating his potato. It was either very hot or he didn't have any teeth!

He just sat slowly nibbling and chewing, watching the goings on in the street. I'd seen him do this for a few days now, poor bugger, the potato was probably the only meal he'd eat all day. I often thought of taking out a pot of cawl or a couple of pies to him but I couldn't of course. I'd have a mob of the poor folk at my door. It was different with poor Polly, she knew to keep her mouth shut, eat the soup out of the pot quickly and not attract attention. Bless her, who'd have thought she'd end up like she did? The old man finished his potato and pulling his cap further down over his forehead and his jacket collar up he crossed the road. He stood outside the cafe door. What the hell was he doing? I couldn't see his face properly because of the pulled down cap and then he shuffled off down the street. Looking for a bit of warmth perhaps but I couldn't have let him in despite my willingness to do so, he was filthy.

Jack came bounding into the shop, he seemed to be in much better spirits these days as were we all. There had been no further murders and a sense of semi normality was returning.

Mary was still very subdued, as was Michael, but neither were the nervous wrecks that they were just a few weeks ago.

"Rees, I hope the murderer is done and gone. My lads on the patrols haven't noticed anything out of the ordinary. All is quiet on the western front as they say. What was the dirty old soak doing outside of the door? Not taking a piss I hope!"

"No, Jack, looking for a bit of warmth I think. He's been around for a few days now. Gets a potato from the stall over the road, sits down on that step", I pointed at the step, "and just watches the world go by as he eats it. Poor old sod! I wish I could let him in but that wouldn't be a wise move, they'd all be wanting in if I did."

"You remember it's the Lord Mayors Day in a couple of weeks, Rees. If I was you I'd get one of those mobile shops or maybe two and set them up along the route. You'll make some serious money I can tell you."

"No doubt that I would, Jack, but we can hardly keep up with demand as it is. Its only one day and I don't think it wouldn't be worth the expense. But thanks anyway."

He shrugged his large shoulders "Just and idea. I'll have a bowl of your delicious soup, if I can find somewhere to sit that is!"

The cafe area was full, the only seat available was a stool by the window where a small shelf was attached to the sill. It was meant to be a table for one but no one ever used it. Jack got his bowl of Cawl and made his way over to the window, setting his bowl down on the little shelf he mounted the stool.

Jack is a large man, it is a small stool, the two did not combine. Jack fell off the stool backwards and landed with a gentle thud on to the flag stone floor! He scrambled to his feet as the sound of laughter erupted in the cafe.

His face was red and full of anger. He picked up the stool held it aloft and I'm sure he would have thrown it through the window if I hadn't shouted out.

"JACK!"

He looked at me, smiled and put the stool back down.

"Rees, I need a bigger stool, my arse don't fit on this one!" The laughter got louder and Jack did a bow to the crowd. Christ! Talk about a Jekyll and Hyde character.

A man motioned to Jack to come and sit in the chair he was vacating as he'd finished his meal and was leaving. The cafe soon quietened down to the normal buzz of conversation. Jack finished his cawl and brought the empty bowl back and placed it on the counter.

"Sorry about that, Rees. It was the shock you see, one minute I'm sat on the stool next thing I'm arse kissing the bloody floor!" He did look very apologetic and a little ashamed.

"No worries, Jack. At least I've still got my window!" I gave him what I hoped was a friendly smile.

"See you later, Rees." he said as he turned to leave.

"Rees, we need to restock the vegetables. You'd better get down the market." Mary called out from the kitchen.

"OK, send Michael out to see to the shop while I'm gone."

Removing my apron and putting on my over coat I left the cafe and made my way to Spitalfields market. I like the market all manner of vegetables and fruits for sale there from all over the world brought in via the docks. How they keep the fruit fresh is a mystery to me.

Traders and buyers were busy bantering, all looking for a good deal. After three years I had my sellers well versed in what was needed. A simple nod as I passed was enough to secure the order and its delivery. What I found refreshing was that the conversations had switched from those 'orrible murders to the more normal, hello, how are you? Sort of talk. I marvelled at Christchurch, designed by William Hawksmoor and built over a century ago. I looked up at its spire reaching toward the sky.

Many of the destitute and addicted folk slept in its grounds. The place where they slept was known as 'Itchy Park' on account of the lice that many of the folk had that caused them to itch and scratch.

I thought about popping into see Jack as Dorset Street was next door but decided against it. I should head back to The Welshman, poor Michael may be run off his feet. If all went as it usually did then my goods would be delivered in the late afternoon and I'd need him to help me put them into the store room.

As I approached the corner of Cable street on which; The Welshman stood I noticed the old man again. He was leaning against the building on the opposite corner, again with his cap pulled down and his jacket collar turned up.

He seemed to be looking at what was going on inside. I quickly made my way towards him but he noticed my approach and took off at a much faster pace than I expected. Who was this man and what was he up to?

"Everything alright, Michael?" I asked as I walked in.

"Yes, Rees, been busy but I coped. You're going to need more candles soon, nearly sold out we have."

"We'll be having a delivery later so get those muscles ready for real work, Michael." I laughed as he bent his arm to show off his non existent biceps.

The cafe was having one of its very rare calm periods so I went out to the kitchen to see how things were.

"How's thing girls?" I said entering the kitchen.

Mary, Emily and Victoria were stood supping from steaming hot cups of tea.

"Nice to have time for a cuppa." Mary said smiling.

"Better make the most of it, doesn't happen that often, girls."

"You don't need to tell us that, Rees, we are the workers you just prop up the shop counter!" Mary said in a teasing voice, a big smile on her face.

I looked into those beautiful eyes for a little longer than I should have. Mary blushed slightly, smiled coyly and then got back to work.

I returned to my place behind the shop counter feeling happier than I had for a long time. The customers came in and the feeding frenzy began again. Full bowls of cawl and plates of pies taken from the cafe counter to the tables, empty bowls and plates returned to the counter. Mr Murphy entered and came up to the counter.

"I'll have my usual please, Rees and some firewood. Wife's feeling cold so I'll have to get a fire going. Sodding landlord won't fix the chimney so we'll have a room full of smoke in no time. Have to open the window then, sort of defeats the purpose but it'll keep the trouble and strife happy!"

I handed him his tobacco and a bundle of firewood put the coins offered into the till and gave him his change.

"What's up with chimney then, Tommy? Got a birds nest in it?"

"Don't know but it's a bit blocked. Told the landlord about it many times but he don't want to know. As long as he gets his rent he couldn't care less. Anyway I'd better be off, oh, before I go, word is there's a gang of tea leaves in the area so be on your guard. They come every year for Lord Mayors Day, rich pickin's with all the people about."

"Tea leaves?" I asked.

"Bloody 'ell, Rees. How long have you been here? Tea leaves.....thieves!"

"I'll never understand the rhyming slang talk, worse than Welsh it is!"

Tommy smiled and with a nod of the head left the shop and went on his way to fill his living room with smoke!

The delivery cart arrived, loaded with sacks of potatoes, carrots, onions, swedes and trays of leeks. I called Michael and with the help of the driver and his assistant we started to unload the cart. The sacks were too heavy for Michael to handle on his own so I gave him a helping hand.

We man handled the sacks behind the shop counter and dropped them through the trap door into the cellar below. When the cart was fully unloaded I paid the driver and his assistant a shilling each. With a grateful thank you they drove off back to the market, the cart horse dropping a pile of shit in to the road as they did so.

The old man watched the activity from his vantage point in the doorway of a building a few doors down. His cap pulled down and an old piece of tarpaulin wrapped around him. Just another bum seeking shelter from the cold. There must be a lot of money held in that place he thought. As the cart passed him he stepped out of the doorway and shuffled off down the street.

Down in the dim lit cellar Michael and I moved the sacks of vegetables over to the far side away from the dirty coal. I'd built large wooden trays to hold the vegetables. Michael cut open the potato sacks and I poured their contents into the tray. The same procedure followed for the onions, swedes and carrots. The coolness and darkness of the cellar would ensure that they stayed fresh for the short while they would be stored there.

The last of the customers left at closing time. Mrs Maxwell turned up as she usually did just before the front door was locked.

"Afternoon, Rees. I'll give a hand with the cleaning up in the kitchen then."

"Yes, thank you, Mrs Maxwell. That will be a great help as always."

"Think nothing of it, I like to be busy, good for the soul it is."

Our little exchange had become a sort of ritual, it was nearly almost the same conversation every afternoon when she came in. She always helped Mary clean up the kitchen at the end of the working day. And it was Thursday, Mary always had a bath on a Thursday evening. I'd be banished to the upstairs living room until Mary was decent again.....the hardships of life!

I locked the front door and started cleaning up the shop area. It wasn't very dirty behind the counter just dropped tea leaves scattered about. The shop floor and that of the cafe were a different matter.

The soles of the shoes of many a customer had painted the floor surface with a mixture of mud, horse shit and god knows what else. An hour or so of hard scrubbing and mopping to get it clean again. Six evenings a week I did the same, scrubbing and mopping. You'd think after all this time that I'd be used to it, not on your Nelly! Putting the mop and bucket back in the shed in the yard I pulled out the tin bath and the two buckets. Placing the bath in the now clean kitchen I went out and filled the two buckets and then placed them on the stove to heat up.

I had to poke the coals a bit to get some life back into the fire. Making sure that the back door was securely locked I went upstairs.

"Mary, the bath is out and the water is on the stove."

"OK, thank you, Rees."

In the living room I lit the fire and watched as the sticks of wood burned with a yellow flame that turned blue where it played around the lumps of coal. Satisfied that a warm fire would soon be burning I settled into the armchair and picked up my book, Daniel Defoe: Robin Crusoe.

My little escape to that desert island in the middle of nowhere, an island where Robinson fights to survive, only to discover that it was too dark to make out the words! Getting up I lit the lamp, turned up the flame and settled once more into the armchair.

Where, after reading a page or two, I dozed off.

I was awakened from my nap by a knock on the living room door.

"Rees, you awake?" Mary quietly asked.

"I am now! Time for tea and biscuits is it?"

Tea and biscuits had become an evening tradition, where we all sat around the fire and talked the mundane talk of life in; The Welshman. The people, what they talked about, how hard they'd worked, just your normal conversation.

"I'll go down and make a pot of tea shall I?" Why I always asked was a bit stupid, I always made the tea in the evening!

In the kitchen I lit the gas lamp. The tin bath was propped up against the wall waiting for me to put it away.

The fire in the stove was a dull ashen pink glow. I put a few lumps of coal on it and went out to put the bath away and fill the kettle from the outside tap. Indoor plumbing would make life a lot easier but in these old buildings it was a rarity. The kettle made a dull clanging noise as I clumsily placed it on the grid over the fire. The tea pot, with the required amount of tea in it awaited the boiled water. Cups and saucers placed on a tray awaited the tea pot. I waited for them all. After what seemed like hours but was only a few minutes the kettle boiled, the teapot was filled and took its place on the tray. I locked the back door and lighting the candle that was fastened to the tray I turned off the lamp and carefully made my way upstairs.

Outside, huddled in the shadows, a pair of eyes watched the candle lit form of Rees ascending the stairs. Looking up at the top window he could see the flickering light of the gas lamp playing against the curtains. It shouldn't be too long before all will be in darkness, I've waited this long, I can wait a little longer he thought.

Rees knocked the tray against the living room door and Mary opened it. She looked radiant after her bath, he hadn't noticed before. He must looked at her too intently as Mrs Maxwell cleared her throat. "Come on then, Rees, put the tray on the table and pour the tea. It won't do it itself!"

"Right you are, Mrs Maxwell. Milk and sugar for all and a couple of biscuits as usual".

We sat around the fire, drinking tea and nibbling biscuits, the conversation being what it normally was. When the talking lulled we all seemed drawn to the flames dancing in the fire, parading their yellow and blue coloured veils for all to see.

The tea and biscuits finished and the sound of yawns began to fill the room, it was time to retire to bed. Cups and saucers placed back on the tray ready for me to take down in the morning. I always got up first as it was my job to light the fire in the kitchen stove.

"Good Night, Rees." Mary said smiling. "Good Night, Mary."

"Good Night." Said Mrs Maxwell and Michael in unison.

 The living room was silent and empty. Lighting the candle on the tray I turned off the lamp, settled down in my chair and decided to read a little more before putting my 'bed' together. The sounds from the bedroom soon quietened as sleep took its occupants off to a different world.

 It wasn't long before my eyes started to close, getting up I pushed the two armchairs together, blew out the candle and jumped into my strange bed. It was surprisingly comfortable and I was soon sleeping.

He watched from the shadows as the light at the window turned to blackness. Good, in an hour or so and it should be safe. He fished around in his filthy waistcoat pocket and then remembered he'd sold his pocket watch a few weeks ago. Damn these people walking about, go home! He waited, watching as the street began to empty, only a few stragglers about now. He smiled, soon, very soon. He felt the excitement bloom inside his wretched body.

The street was quiet apart from the ladies of the night that could be seen as shadows in the murky darkness away from the gas lamps. Ghosts of the night might be a better description.

That was good because he would be seen only as a shadow himself or perhaps not seen at all. Leaving his hide away he crossed the street and approached the front door of; The Welshman.

His rather brief but very informative examination of the lock earlier that afternoon, told him what lock it was and what was needed to open it. Reaching into a dirty, very frayed jacket pocket he produced a large key ring from which many keys hung. Carefully he tried the keys one by one until, with a gentle click the lock disengaged. Turning the door handle he gently pushed and opened the door. The freshly oiled hinges didn't make a sound. Entering the shop area he pushed the door shut with his foot and made for the passageway that he could just see in the gloom. His days of surveillance having paid off as he knew where to go. What he hadn't noticed was that the front door was not fully shut, the latch had clicked but not engaged and the door was slightly open. Very slowly he climbed the stairs, being careful where he trod.

Standing on the landing he looked through the semi-darkness at the doors leading off it. This was unfamiliar territory. He slowly opened the first door to his left and peeped around it into the room beyond. He could just make out three sleeping forms. This was the room he wanted!

In a world far away someone gave a muffled scream, I heard the thump of something falling to the floor. As I slowly awoke the shout of "DON'T STRUGGLE." brought me fully awake. What the hell is going on? Forgetting my make shift 'bed' I fell out of it in my haste to get up.

"REES!......... REES!......... I'VE GOT A SUPRISE FOR YOU!"

A strange but yet vaguely familiar voice cried out.

Scrambling to my feet I rushed out of the living room, the door banging against the wall as I did so.

Diving across the landing I barrelled into the bedroom opposite. The glare from the lamp temporarily blinding me. Once my eyes had accustomed to the brightness the sight that greeted me was one of sheer terror. The old man I had so often seen in the street was standing behind Mary, one hand over her mouth the other holding a knife to her throat! Mrs Maxwell was on the floor by the wall. I don't know if she's alive or dead. Michael lay on the cot a huge bruise growing on the side of his face, his jaw looked broken.

Instantly enraged I moved forward.

"STAY BACK! or I swear I'll cut her throat!"

The look of madness in his eyes told me that he would do it. I looked at Mary, she was terrified, her eyes wide and staring. He looked very familiar, there was something about the face, and the voice. Who the hell does he remind me of?

" Don't you know me?"

No, I didn't know him. All I knew was that I wanted to kill the bastard!

"Shall I give you a clue? You need a clue? Look at me closely."

As I looked at him an image formed in my mind, but it couldn't be the man I saw. He had lost a lot of weight. His face was gaunt. He was absolutely filthy and the stench coming off him would have normally turned my stomach but the adrenalin marching through my veins was counteracting the urge to heave. No it couldn't be! But there could be no mistaking the identity of the man stood with a knife to my Mary's throat. It was John Kelly!

"John, what the hell are you doing man? Have you completely lost your mind? I don't understand. Please, John, I beg you don't hurt her, please don't hurt her." I pleaded. I looked at Mary and my heart broke.

"Sit down on the floor, over there in the corner. There's a lot you need to know before I'm finished." He said in a very menacing tone.

"You must have wondered over the years what happened to your mother, Rees. Why she suddenly disappeared and where did she go?"

He knew my name! That was the absolute confirmation, it was was Kelly. I nodded unable to speak my anger having given way to despair.

"Well you see, Rees, I always fancied her, fine looking woman she was. I used to go into the shop and flirt with her, only she wasn't interested, in fact I could see by the look on her face that she didn't like me much. And your grandfather, the bastard, made it very clear that I was to stop my 'harassment' of your mother, to use his words."

Mrs Maxwell gave a groan but didn't move.

"I didn't lay a finger on her, she collapsed when she saw me and hasn't moved since."

"What have you done to Michael, you bastard?"

"That little runt came flying at me so I popped him one on the jaw! Went down like a sack of shit he did!" He smiled as he said it.

" HE'S JUST A BOY!" I shouted.

"Do I look as I give a fuck, Rees? Didn't want him spoiling my plans now did I."

I looked down at the floor, seeing the hopeless look in Mary's eyes was too much for me.

"Where was I? Oh, yes. I'd sit in the cafe over the road and watch the shop. I soon learned that your grandfather left the shop every Wednesday morning and was gone until early afternoon, leaving your mother on her own."

Shifting position slightly he continued.

" I waited for him to leave one Wednesday morning, watching him make his way up Wood field Street. I left the cafe and went into the shop. Your mother's face was a picture, Rees. She really didn't want me in there. I had a look through the window at what was going on outside, nothing much, the people just going about their business. I locked the door, Rees. Your mother moved into the back of the shop, she was scared, really scared. That just added to my enjoyment!"

I started to get up.

"THAT WOULD NOT BE WISE!" John shouted and drew the knife slowly across Mary's neck. A small dribble of blood ran from beneath it's blade and down her throat.

"OK, John, look I'm sitting down, see, sitting down." My heart was pounding in my chest. Mary's face was a mask of abject terror.

"Good boy, Rees. As I was saying, she kept backing away, pleading with me all the while, No, John, please, John. I was loving it. We ended up in the kitchen where I saw the table. I backed her up against it and then pushed her over it. Oh, she tried to scream but I just squeezed her throat until she stopped. I eased up her skirts , ripped her stays off and took her there and then, Rees, loved it she did!"

I kept my eyes firmly locked on Mary. I had to or I would be the cause of her death. The rage within me was intolerable! This had to be a very bad dream. A nightmare to beat all nightmares!

"She couldn't tell anyone, Rees. It was perfect! Respectable married woman and all is not going to tell. The shame of it, can you imagine? I lost interest in her after that, she was soiled goods in my eyes. I still went to the shop but the flirting stopped. Your fucking grandfather suspected something, I know he did but he said nothing. He just treated me with total disdain but I could live with that."

A noise outside caught his attention. It was only the cackle of a drunken man finding his way home but it distracted the thought of the maddened, John. He pulled Mary even closer as his fevered brain tried to recollect where it was.

"Yes, the perfect crime. She came to me a few weeks later. Sought me out in the Prince Albert pub. She actually came into the pub, how the mighty had fallen, Rees. Your mother going into a public unaccompanied, the shame, Rees, the shame! She calls me outside and tells me she is with child and that the child is mine! I laughed at her, Rees, can you imagine that. A married woman tells me that and expects me to believe it! I smacked her and knocked her to the ground!"

"You worthless piece of shit! Somebody must have noticed that! Wait, she was pregnant? That means I have a......."

"Yes, Rees, but I'll get to that later." He coughed and then continued.

"Nobody noticed, Rees, and if they did then they kept it to themselves. You always were an innocent prick, Mr fucking do-gooder. See no evil, Rees, that was the code. Ah, but it gets better, Rees, much better. Your mother then tells me that it couldn't be your dads because they were waiting until you were a little older before adding to the family. We just did different things to please each other she told me. Ha! I was going to be a dad!"

I brought my knees up to my chest and hugged them, trying to gain some comfort. This just couldn't be true, not my mother, he's confused in his madness.

"I've never know a woman to beg as she did, Rees. She begged me to help her get away to save your dad and you from the shame. My husband will know that the child is not his she said. I think she was losing it a bit, you know, in her head." He laughed at what he thought was funny.

"So, that's what I did, Rees. I arranged for her to come to London, Docklands to be exact, certain friends of mine helped out and kept an eye on her, just to make sure."

Mary made muffled noises behind the filthy hand that was clamped over her mouth. John pressed the knife harder against her neck causing another trickle of blood to flow.

"It was alright until the baby was born and then things started going bad. She couldn't work because of the baby so she got herself mixed up with a few of the local whores and became one herself. And that was the beginning of the end. They'd take it in turns to work the streets while one always looked after the baby. I see from your look, Rees, that you are wondering how I know all this? I still had friends in the East End and they kept me informed of the situation and my daughters progress. I visited a few times, oh, not in person, watched from a distance and I didn't like what I saw. Your mother was a shambling, drunken wreck. Her so called slut friends were the same and in the middle of it all was my daughter!"

"I have a sister?" I feebly asked. Too stunned to think properly.

He ignored my question and stopped talking. He appeared to be trying to calm himself. Mary stared straight ahead, unblinking, afraid to move a muscle.

"But I slowly lost interest, time and distance and all that. Morriston was my home and its people my friends. I decided to forget that I had a daughter and get on with my life."

"YOU RAPED MY MOTHER! JOHN. YOU WERE THE REASON SHE LEFT US! YOU BASTARD!" I was screaming, my rage over powering my reasoning.

"And all those years you knew and said nothing!" I said, forcing myself to calm down.

"Of course I didn't, Rees. That was my power, knowing what the rest of you didn't. I thought I played the part of a concerned citizen very well. Although you won't remember that, still shitting in your nappy you were then!" John said in a smug tone.

"Me and Jack had a long conversation about you. Jack told me all about your trouble here and how you had to leave. Did you honestly think that he wouldn't after you conned the both of us? If Jack finds you, he will kill you, John! And given the chance so will I!"

If looks could kill then I'd be a dead man. Don't push him any further, Rees, I thought to myself.

"Twenty years, Rees. Twenty fucking years I stayed clear of the card tables! Until that night in the Red Lion, I had a few beers too many see. A game was set up in the back room. I'll just watch them play, that's what I told myself. Well, it wasn't long and I was playing hard and losing fast. They were professional players, the sum of money in the pot was hundreds of pounds. I soon owed a lot of money, over a hundred pounds, money I didn't have. And, as happened all those years before, it was made very clear to me what would happen if I didn't pay the debt."

He was getting very worked up, the muscles in his face twitching, the hand holding the knife trembling. I hoped it wouldn't slip!

"I stole a few quid from the firm, not all at once and not too much, I'd learned that lesson. It was enough to keep them off my back but they wanted all what I owed or I'd be tied up, large stones placed in my clothing and I'd be thrown into the Tawe alive! Motivates a man that does, Rees."

He coughed and spittle dribbled down his chin.

"Then you tell me you wanted to sell up and move on. Bingo! There was my way out! I spun you the yarn about Jack. I had to make it sound convincing didn't I even if it was a load of fucking shit. The job I pulled on your solicitor, that was a beauty. He didn't have a fucking clue, not one."

He coughed again, a bronchial cough that didn't sound too good.

"My forgery skills are still good, a few shillings spent here and there got me the official water marked paper that solicitors and the like always look for. The London solicitors was a gem, it was a post office box address. I simply went up to London, retrieved the correspondence and sent the confirmation back. That's why I was away on business see, Rees, got to do these things properly."

Now he was smiling, showing his putrid unclean teeth. He's totally insane, that was obvious.

"Then it all went wrong. My thefts were discovered and I was dismissed from my employment. They do say that history repeats itself. Without a job I couldn't pay my rent or anything. I was a respected man in Morriston, Rees, I couldn't rely on charity.

So, with no other choice I got into another card game, my luck had to get better. It fucking didn't! I lost my remaining few pounds and a hell of lot more I didn't have. I was back in the shit again!"

I looked at him with feigned sympathy. He could flip at any time and if he did Mary was dead.

" I came back to Spitalfields. My old friends would help me out or so I thought. No, they fucking didn't. Word had got around that I'd conned Jack and I was told to leave in no uncertain terms. I had no where to go so I hid, kept off the main streets and lived like a gutter urchin. I've lived like that for months now, Rees. Look at the state of me! I even had to sell my pocket watch, been in the family for generations that has. I saw you many times, Rees, in your fancy fucking cafe. I noticed Mary too."

He looked down at Mary, playing the knife gently across her throat.

"Such a sweet young thing and smelling of bath lavender. It must be nice to have a bath. I haven't had one for months, gets a man down it does."

My heart was now hammering away in my chest. I must get him out of the self pity mood, that could be bloody dangerous!

"You can have a bath here, John. Just let Mary go, there's no real harm done yet. I'll get you some clean clothes and money, I have lots of money, you can have it all!"

"If only it were that simple, Rees. I'm afraid its gone too far for such a simple solution."

Tightening his grip on Mary's mouth he moved the knife down to the buttons on the front of her dressing gown and with a sudden downwards thrust of the knife he cut a tear from the neckline to the midsection! I jumped up.

John let out an animal like growl that stopped me in my tracks. His eyes were glazed and quite mad.

I feared that Mary would very soon be dead. Placing the knife behind the torn cloth he moved it aside to reveal a milky white breast and pink nipple.

"Lovely isn't she, Rees. Clean and fresh, a work of art. She is perfection."

He was ranting, his brain had finally given way. All hope drained from me. All I could pray for was a quick death for us all. Mary had gone into shock. Her eyes unfocused, her body as stiff as a board.

"You see, Rees, I spent a lot of time watching what went on here, the people coming and going. That bastard, Jack among them. And one of the sluts from all those years ago, one of your mothers old friends."

I didn't realise that he had started talking again I was waiting for the killing blow to be struck.

"I got talking to her, shared some rum with her, soon loosened her tongue that did. What she told me was very interesting."

Releasing Mary's mouth, she said nothing, he reached inside his jacket and pulled out a torn photograph which he threw to me.

"Recognise her do you, Rees?"

I looked at the torn photograph it was of a young woman, very attractive and nicely dressed in a flowing gown.

"No, I don't think so. Who is she?" I was playing for time, I don't care who she is!

"You really don't recognise your own mother, Rees? Now that is shameful."

I looked at him and than back at the photograph. Was this my mother?

"It is her, Rees. I took it off the window sill by the table in the kitchen when I had my bit of fun with her. Your dad was on the other part but I tore him off. A souvenir of my conquest you could say. Every time I look at it I remember what it felt like to thrust into her, even after all these years."

Why hadn't my grandfather never mentioned the picture or its loss? That didn't make sense.

"I know what you're thinking, I'd be thinking the same. I knew that your mother would clear it all up, hide the evidence. She probably invented a believable story about the missing picture. But your grandfather wasn't a stupid man, not by a long shot, and that's why I think he suspected me."

There could be no doubt as to his madness or his cunning. I looked at Mary she was still catatonic, I glanced at her exposed breast and quickly looked away. I have to save her but how?

"The slut I talked to was Polly Nichols and before she died she told me something that made my hair stand on end. She also told me where to find the others. Except for the one in Berner Street that was a special present to a special person!"

I looked at him in total disbelief and was instantly filled with a feeling of sheer dread. This can't be happening. John Kelly was the tabloids ; Jack The Ripper!

"YOU! killed those poor women?"

"YES, REES! I killed them all. The sluts that were the friends of another slut. But that isn't all. I did wonder what happened to my daughter over the years. Was she alive, was she dead? I didn't know either way until I spoke to that slut Nichols"

"But why kill them, John. Why?"

"WHY? YOU ASK ME WHY? YOU HAVE IT ALL, REES. I HAVE NOTHING!" He screamed at me.

"AND THIS BITCH IS BETTER OFF THAN I AM, THAT'S NOT RIGHT, REES!" As he screamed the spittle flew from his lips.

He caressed Mary's exposed breast and then grabbed it hard. Mary didn't flinch.

"You see, Rees" He said in a much calmer voice.

" Mary is my DAUGHTER and your SISTER!"

The world swam before me as the blood drained from my head I was going to black out.

"Stay with me, Rees. Look at the photograph of your mother and then look at Mary."

I looked at the image of my mother and then at Mary, there could be no denying the likeness between them. The same shaped face, the little pert nose, the full lips and that abundant glossy hair.

John moved his face next to Mary's.

"Look at our eyes, Rees. What do you see?"

I saw the same eyes. Two pairs of identical, almond shaped, steel grey eyes. And then the penny dropped that's where I had seen Mary's eyes before. They were exactly the same as those of John fucking Kelly!

"YOU BLAME US FOR WHAT HAPPENED? YOU'RE MAD, JOHN!" It was my turn to scream.

I looked at Mary, her eyes were focused! She was back in the land of reality!

What happened next was a blur. Mary turned her head quickly and bit into John's face. The blood erupted and Mary spat a lump of flesh onto the floor. John howled in pain, dropping the knife, his hands clutching at his cheek. The knife fell to the floor at the side of the cot.

Mary ran to me as John reached down for the knife. Michael rolled over grabbed the knife and thrust it into Johns descending throat! He staggered and then stood upright, the knife buried up to the hilt and protruding out of the back of his neck. He looked at Mary and me and then the light in his steel grey eyes went out. His knees buckled and he was dead before he hit the floor.

Mary clung to me as if her life depended on it. Michael climbed in between us and the three of us sat on the floor, scared and in shock. Mrs Maxwell hadn't moved but I could see that she was still breathing.

Jack and a couple of his men were patrolling the street. As they passed the cafe one of them stopped.

"Jack, the doors open." Phil said.

Jack pushed the door and motioning for his men to follow he entered.

"REES, ARE YOU ALRIGHT?" he shouted.

"NO JACK, GET UP HERE QUICK!" I shouted back.

The sound of thudding up the steps was deafening. Jack burst into the room and stopped dead in his tracks. Phil and Mike behind him.

"What the fuck happened here?" Jack asked, looking at Kelly's dead body.

"Who is that bum?"

"Look at him, Jack, look closely, it's John Kelly. He's the killer!"

Jack looked as if he'd swallowed a hot pepper. His face crimson red his eyes watering with rage.

"That piece of shit is the killer? He never had the guts to squash a fly the cowardly bastard!"

"You haven't heard the best yet but it will have to wait. Better get the police, Jack."

"Are you nuts, Rees? No police. If word of this gets out you won't sell a tea leaf again let alone anything else. And you'll be plagued by the ghouls wanting to see where Jack The Ripper died. The press will hound you wherever you go. These murders have been reported about world wide, can you imagine it, Rees? There would be no peace for you. They'd find you where ever you went. Who stuck the fucker?"

"Michael did, Jack. I've never seen a person move so fast."

"You'd be surprised what people can do when they have to."

Turning to Mary he couldn't help but notice that she was a little over exposed. Taking off his jacket he handed it to her. She covered herself and thanked him with a very tired smile but at least it was a smile.

He told Phil and Mike to go and get a travelling trunk and be quick about it. Leaning over Mrs Maxwell he felt her throat and listened to her chest.

"I'm no doctor but her pulse is strong and her breathing is regular. She must have had a fit or something."

A short while later Phil and Mike returned with the travelling trunk. Mary changed into a fresh dressing gown , she turned her back to us to do so and we all looked away. Despite the horror of the situation modesty still had its place. She handed Jack his jacket and went with Michael into the living room. Jack and his men picked up Kelly's body, bent in half and placed in the trunk. Bleach and soap took care of the blood stains and the smell.

"We'll take care of this, Rees, and there's a doctor on the way. Don't worry, he's one of mine, won't ask any questions. That's what I pay him for."

The trunk was manhandled down the stairs and off to god knows where. I didn't ask and Jack didn't say.

Mary, Michael and myself were sitting in the living room. Me in one armchair and Mary in the other with Michael sat on her lap. The doctor had been and gone. Mary's throat was not badly injured just a few light cuts. Michael's jaw was not broken but very badly bruised. Poor Mrs Maxwell had been transported to the hospital as the doctor thought she may have had a stroke.

"Rees, how do you feel.......about......."

"About our mother and the fact that you are my half sister? Shocked and sad. I love you, Mary, in the way that a man should love a woman. And when I realised what that bastard Kelly said is true, my heart broke." I paused, over whelmed by sadness.

"It will take me a while to get over it, it will be the same for us all. But at least I have a sister and nephew that I didn't know I had. That makes it easier to bear." I gave the best smile that I could manage.

"I know exactly how you feel, Rees." she said as the tears rolled down her cheeks.

The laudanum mixture the doctor had given Michael was taking effect. Mary made him comfortable in the chair and went to sit at the table.

"Rees, this did really happen didn't it, it's not some bad dream that we'll wake up from is it?"

I shook my head. How I wished it was!

"I don't understand why my mother.....sorry.....our mother, lied to me. Why all that nonsense about Cardiff and how the family threw her out?"

"She had her reasons, Mary. Maybe just to confuse her history to protect you. She would have done that. She left my dad and me for the same reason, to protect us."

Mary nodded but said nothing.

The morning light awoke me from my fitful slumber. Mary was curled up on the chair with Michael. I quietly went down stairs and wrote on a plywood board in chalk: The Welshman will be closed until further notice. Placing the board in the window I made my way to the kitchen to make a pot of tea. The table that my mother had been violated on stood under the window.

I no longer saw my grandfather rolling out his pastry on it. The image was replaced by Kelly brutally raping my mother! The table would have to go whether I stayed or not.

I took the tray with the tea pot, cups and saucers upstairs and left them on the living room table. Mary was awake and smiled at me, still too sleep addled to do much more. Downstairs I sat on the stool behind the counter trying to make sense of what had happened. Only, there was no sense to it at all. I knew that the police should be informed. The killer had been hunted for weeks and we knew who he was. But Jack was right.

We'd be hounded by the press, pursued by the people where ever we went and constantly hunted and hounded by the macabre wishing to view the site where the ripper died. Let sleeping dogs lie. I looked up as someone knocked on the door. Relief flooded through me as I saw it was Jack. I let him in. He didn't look very happy but then none of us did.

"Mornin', Rees, not that it is. I just wanted you to know that all business has been taken care of. I've spoken to the doctor, Mrs Maxwell is awake but can't remember anything. Damned fortunate is that."

"I'm glad of that, Jack, it's for the better, for her at least."

"So, have you had any thoughts on what you're going to do now?" Jack asked.

"I think I'll take Mary and Michael back to Swansea for a little while. Show them where their roots lie and to get them away from here. And to be honest, Jack, I don't think I'll get any arguments."

I looked down at the floor and then back at Jack. He must have noticed something was wrong, he new how to read people.

"Better tell me what's bothering you, Rees. A trouble shared and all that."

I told him everything as Kelly had explained it. I didn't stop for breath just kept on going until all of it was said. When I had finished the big bull of a man had the look of a lost child.

"Jack, for years I had a sister I didn't know about. And then to find out that she is the woman I love.....it hurts, Jack, it really hurts."

"Fuck Me! That fuckin' bastard! I should have left him out in the open so the crows could peck his fuckin' eyes out! Perhaps getting away from here is the best thing. Don't worry about The Welshman. It will be looked after."

I nodded my head, knowing that he meant every word.

The next few days were spent trying to get some normality back into our shattered lives. Michael, surprisingly, was back to his old self.

His bruises were fading as were his memories, or so it appeared. Mary and I were getting along, now as brother sister and not as potential lovers. We had all agreed that a holiday in Swansea would do us all good. Mary really wanted to see where her 'family' came from.

Our trunks were all packed and waiting to be picked up. Mary, Michael and myself were going to spend some time in a guest house near to Caswell Bay on the Gower coast.

Jack was in the kitchen where Emily and Victoria were instructing him on how things worked. I looked in and I have to say that he didn't look too happy.

The carriage pulled up and the driver and his cab man started loading our trunks. Mary and Michael having said their good byes to Jack, excitedly climbed aboard the carriage. I waited until all the commotion was over. Jack sauntered over to me and held out his huge paw which I willingly shook.

"Rees, I'm just a bit curious so don't answer if you don't want to. What was your mother's name?"

Releasing his hand and turning toward the carriage I said.

"Her name was Mary."

The End

Printed in Poland
by Amazon Fulfillment
Poland Sp. z o.o., Wrocław